LAUREN DANE

Cascadia
Wolves
Tri Mates

ELLORA'S CAVE
ROMANTICA®
WWW.ELLORASCAVE.COM

An Ellora's Cave Publication

www.ellorascave.com

Tri Mates

ISBN 9781419964046
ALL RIGHTS RESERVED.
Tri Mates Copyright © 2006 Lauren Dane
Edited by Ann Leveille.
Cover art by Syneca.

Electronic book publication November 2006
Trade paperback publication 2011

TRI MATES

ஐ

Dedication

૭૭

Yep — Ray, you're it. Now and always. Thank you for giving me a great model for these sexy and wonderful heroes.

My beta readers, Julia and Tracy, this one is better because of you guys. Thank you!

No dedication is complete without thanking Ann Leveille, who makes me mind my grammar manners and whips me into shape and my books too. Thank you, Ann.

Trademarks Acknowledgement

ဆ

The author acknowledges the trademarked status and trademark owners of the following wordmarks mentioned in this work of fiction:

Architectural Digest: Advance Magazine Publishers Inc.

BMW: Bayerische Motoren Werke Aktiengesellschaft

Cadillac: General Motors Corporation

Craigslist: CRAIGSLIST, INC. CORPORATION

Doc Martens: Dr. Martens International Trading GmbH

Godiva: Godiva Brands, Inc.

Hot Topic: Hot Topic, Inc.

Jones New York: Jones Investment Co. Inc.

Mercedes–Benz: DaimlerChrysler AG CORPORATION

NASCAR: National Association for Stock Car Auto Racing, Inc.

Porsche: Dr. Ing. h.c. F. Porsche Aktiengesellschaft CORPORATION

Portland Trail Blazers: Trail Blazers, Inc.

Red Sox: Boston Red Sox Baseball Club Limited Partnership

Sub-Zero: SUB-ZERO FREEZER COMPANY, INC.

Subaru Outback: FUJI JUKOGYO KABUSHIKI KAISHA TA Fuji Heavy Industries Ltd.

Chapter One

ഔ

Tracy Warden grabbed a cup of coffee in the spacious kitchen belonging to her brothers and sister-in-law. It was a room that felt like home. A room she'd cooked numerous meals in, had shared coffee and drinks in with her sister-in-law and best friend, Nina. Before Nina came, the room—the house—had been nice enough, but somehow the love she brought, the laughter and joy, made it a home.

Tracy often wondered if it was about Nina or the connection she had with Lex. Wondered if she'd ever have that sense of belonging in a place—to someone—that Nina and Lex obviously did.

"Have some breakfast, Trace. There's plenty. You know how Cade is when he cooks. He'll pout like a four-year-old if you don't eat anything."

She looked back over her shoulder at Nina and laughed at the irreverence with which her sister-in-law treated their Alpha and the oldest brother in the Warden family. Cade may have scared the bejesus out of everyone else but Nina was fearless. Of course, considering the last year and a half of Nina's life, what did she have to fear that she hadn't overcome?

"You're going to get me into trouble, old woman," Tracy snickered as she joined Nina at the table.

"If you think I didn't hear that comment, Nina, you're mistaken," Cade said in a growl as he came into the room and put a platter of bacon and another of eggs and toast down.

"Oh I'm all aquiver. I beg your pardon, Oh Supreme Tool, er, Alpha. Please don't discipline me with your scary frown and spatula."

9

Lex came in, kissed the top of Nina's head and sat down, trying to stifle his smile.

"He needs to take you in hand," Cade groused as he sat and began to heap food on his plate.

"Oh he has. Can't you recognize the satisfied look on his face?" Nina said, one eyebrow up as she put a napkin on her lap.

"TMI! Let's talk about something else, please, while I still have an appetite," Tracy joked as she buttered her toast.

"TMI?" Lex looked puzzled.

"Too much information." Nina winked at her sister-in-law.

"Yes, like how Mom keeps coming over here looking for you, Tracy. She says you're never home. Are you ducking her?" Cade had his big-brother-Alpha face on.

"I keep telling you to rekey the gate code so she can't sneak in here," Nina murmured to Lex, who nearly choked on his coffee.

"She'd just climb it, she's ruthless when there's prey in her sights." Lex grinned behind his cup.

Cade looked at Lex and tried not to smile, but lost the battle. "Okay, so she's..."

"Pushy? Come on, Cade! She keeps *dropping in* at my house with werewolves in tow who she just *ran into* at the grocery store or somesuch. It's blatant and annoying. Megan and Tegan just hide from her when she comes over here, Lex married Nina and you, you're the Alpha and she has to be nicer to you so I'm vulnerable to her attacks."

"Don't you want to have someone?" Lex asked quietly, his fingers playing with the ends of Nina's hair.

Tracy softened. "Yes. Yes, I do, Lex. But I don't want to date some suck-up that wants an in with the Alpha's family. I want my mate. I want the kind of connection that you and Nina have."

"Fair enough, doll." Nina reached out and squeezed her hand. "You'll find him. When you least expect it." She grinned then. "And boy is he in for it!"

* * * * *

After breakfast, Tracy went into the office to start the accounting paperwork she did part-time for the Pack business and Nina moved about the house dealing with the plants before she went in to her gardening business for the day. Her florist shop had been burned down a year and a half before and instead of opening another florist's she'd gone and opened up a full-scale nursery on the Eastside that had further nurtured her love for all things green—and had done extremely well in the bargain.

Lex Warden tried not to notice how good his wife looked as she reached up to water the plants on the shelves above the kitchen counter. The morning sun streamed through the window and over her body. Normally she was hard to ignore but this morning it was even worse as her skirt inched up ever higher as she moved.

Seeing the creamy café au lait skin of her thighs reminded him of the particularly fabulous way she'd said good morning and he had to shift in his seat as his cock hardened against the buttons of his fly.

"Hello? You still with us, Lex, or you planning to ravish your wife?" Cade snapped his fingers in front of Lex's face as he followed the direction of Lex's glance. Nina Reyes–Warden was quite a specimen and Cade harbored more than one of his own fantasies about his sister-in-law. He certainly couldn't blame his brother for the goofy, dreamy smile he wore. His brother had been totally head over heels for his mate since the first moment he'd taken a deep whiff of her, and Cade envied that.

Lex snorted as Nina turned and rolled her eyes at both of them. "Jeez! Can't a girl water plants around here without being objectified?" She squirted water at both of them and sashayed out, smiling to herself.

The phone rang and a few moments later Nina walked back into the room and handed the receiver to Lex. "It's the Enforcer from the Pacific Clan."

His fingers brushed hers and he watched, satisfied, as her pupils widened and her breathing sped up. He sent her a cocky grin and she mumbled "fucking furry tease" on her way back out of the room.

Cade motioned that he was going into his office to work and Lex nodded shortly before taking his call.

Lex came into the office half an hour later and threw his long frame into a chair. "That was Nick Lawrence calling about more border bullshit. I've sent Dave down to pick up three of our wolves who're in jail for fighting with Pacific wolves. This dispute has gone on long enough. Someone is going to end up really hurt or dead."

"Call the Mediator. You know it's unavoidable." Cade took a sip of his coffee, chuckling. The National Pack had a mediator, a man who came in to solve inter-Pack disputes. It was a pain to deal with bureaucracy like that, but Alpha wolves made for ridiculously complicated negotiations. It was better to call in an expert before wolves died.

"I know. Better we deal with this now."

Cade nodded. "And anyway, the wolf who's been in the shadow seat was made Mediator three years ago. I hear he's good. Young. Forward-thinking. When you get together, take Nick aside and ask their opinion about the issue of Pellini Group's influence on the National Governance Council."

Lex sighed and finished his coffee. "I can't imagine they like it any more than we do. Most of the Packs don't like it. I say we deal with it now, before they get any more power."

"That's treason and I forbid you to talk like that outside of this house." Cade's voice was sharp. Warren Pellini and his *connected* wolves had found an in into the National Pack governance structure. Right now Pellini had the ear of a few powerful wolves, and they were all uneasy.

"Hey, I can do my fucking job, Cade. You don't need to forbid me like I'm some unranked wolf." Lex pushed his chair back and stood up, eyes flashing.

"Whoa!" Nina rushed into the room and put herself between them. "Knock it off, both of you! You don't see me and Tracy doing this sort of thing, do you?" Nina tossed an annoyed look over her shoulder at her sister-in-law, who was watching the exchange with similar annoyance and concern. "Boys, boys, put your cocks away please. If you don't, I'm just going to break out the ruler and measure them once and for all. But let's do this instead—shut the fuck up and stop the swaggery Who's the Biggest Baddest Wolf crap. At least before lunch."

She placed a hand on each of their chests and felt their pounding hearts beneath her palms. Their hearts in her hand, it meant something. The three of them were tied to each other in a really elemental way and sometimes she was the bridge between two very strong males.

The anger and challenge drained from them and she allowed herself a little sigh of relief.

"God, you're full of shit for someone so hot." Cade leaned in, kissed her forehead and looked around her at his brother. "I didn't mean offense by it. I do trust you to do your job. I trust you with my life every day. This is worrying me more than I realized, I suppose."

Lex relaxed a bit and pulled Nina to him with one hand, her back to his chest, and grabbed his brother with the other and cupped his neck. "Of course. I'm sorry I overreacted."

Tracy snorted. Turning around, she picked up the pile of paper she'd been working on, and put it in front of Cade. "I have to go to work." She shook her head at her sister-in-law. "Better you to have to deal with this crap than me."

"You're going to work dressed like that?" Cade frowned at Tracy in her very short denim skirt, her legs encased in fishnet stockings. She was wearing a tight red sweater and her golden-brown hair hung in loose curls around her face and shoulders.

"No, I forgot my boots." She reached into the hall closet and pulled out a pair of high-heeled boots that laced up the front and came to her knees.

"Holy crap! Trace, you cannot possibly go out in public dressed like that!" Lex narrowed his eyes, hands on his hips as he took his baby sister in.

"Why not? She looks amazing." Nina kissed Tracy's cheek and turned back to look at her husband.

"That's the point. That skirt is too short, the sweater is too tight. The boots, they're...they're..." At a loss for words, Lex just gestured at her wildly.

Tracy winked at both her overbearing brothers and pulled her coat on. "They're really gorgeous, aren't they? I love them." Looking back at Nina, she grinned. "Just call me or have your guy call me and I'll bring those pots back here tonight."

Blowing them all a kiss, she sauntered out of the room, yelled her goodbyes to everyone else and left.

* * * * *

Aside from the accounting work she did for the Pack, Tracy was lucky enough to have the refuge of her record store, Spin the Black Circle. She had loved the place since the first moment she'd found the empty storefront two years before but it was an added bonus that her mother hated it and didn't want to come near it. Tracy was spending a lot of time there lately and was strongly considering kicking out the tenants who lived upstairs so she could move in there and have a great reason to keep her mother away. She was also fortunate to have a manager who loved the store almost as much as she did and who ran the place with amazing efficiency and the help of a small but great staff.

After several hours at the store, she went home to get some paperwork for Cade. The house was one that she'd spent a lot of time in as a kid. Her grandparents had turned the Pack over to her father before Tracy was born, and as a result they had a lot of free time to spend with their grandchildren.

Milton, her chocolate Labrador retriever, was happily waiting for her in the front windows. Those big front windows looked out toward the Ballard Locks. The water could look green and murky, black and cold or bright blue and glittering beneath the sun depending on the day and the season. The small porch had a glider swing and plants that were tended to by Nina. Even in the cold of winter, she'd had colorful plants. Nina planted some stuff that looked like cabbages and they were a vibrant purple. Tracy had no freaking idea just what it was, but she couldn't argue that it made the house look nice with a bit of color to break the monotony of the gray Seattle skies.

The house had been built in the Forties. Architecture of that type was dying in the area, where old houses were being bought and demolished and new ones replaced them. She preferred the old-style charm of the place, the curved doorways and big common areas and small bedrooms. Heck, the house still had the original hardwood floors. Tracy had stripped them down and refinished them herself a few years before.

She smiled to herself as she unlocked the front door and turned the alarm off. It was hers, this place. Filled with memories of weekends walking to nearby Woodland Park Zoo and having picnics. Time spent digging in the dirt with her grandmother, planting bulbs each November. Her father's life had been consumed with the Pack and her grandparents had been a more tangible part of her life than her parents had been for a very long time. More than a few nights of her life it had been her grandfather who'd tucked her into bed and her grandmother who'd baked the snacks for her classroom celebrations. Her mother had been miserable without the presence of her mate and had retreated into herself and into community work for a great many years. Until her father had handed over the leadership of Cascadia to Cade.

Shaking her head to dislodge the memories, she grinned instead at what greeted her. A big overstuffed couch sat across from the fireplace and currently held Milton, who was giving her his lopsided grin, tongue peeking through his front teeth. She rolled her eyes at him and laughed at the sight he made.

It was odd for her to have a dog. Some werewolves didn't have animals because they felt owning animals was exploitative or they were uncomfortable that they too were close to dogs on some level. But Tracy had found Milton at the animal shelter when he was a puppy. She'd fallen in love with him immediately. Most people wouldn't adopt a dog with three legs. But Milton sure wasn't affected by it and she couldn't find a reason not to bring the goofy dog home with her. She hadn't regretted her choice once in the four years he'd been with her.

"Hey, dude." She leaned down and smooched the top of his head. Suppressing a smile, she scratched behind his ears until he made that growly moan, nearly falling over because his one back leg thumped in response.

She laughed and opened up the back door to let him out, tossing his tennis ball for him. She knew the dog walker had been by but he did love a good run out there while she made dinner.

Tossing her coat and scarf on a chair, she put her bag on the hook and took a quick look into the mirror, running fingers through her curly hair.

Big green eyes looked back at her, and an eyebrow ring that should have overwhelmed her face but really just enhanced the pixieish nature of her features. A dusting of freckles sprinkled over her nose and cheeks, the juxtaposition of the eyebrow ring and the row of piercings up each ear and that tiny nose and freckled face worked for her. There was an air of wicked innocence about her. Of mischief.

After a quick change into jeans and wooly socks, she poured food into Milton's bowl and made sure he had fresh water and cooked up a quick stir-fry before she went out to Nina's. She loved these quiet evenings when she wasn't expected at the Pack house, time that was hers alone. She did admit to herself that it would be nice to have a man around. It wasn't like she never dated. She'd just gotten out of a six-month relationship a few weeks prior. The problem was, wolves tended to not get into long-term relationships while they were younger and looking for a mate. She pitied the poor human men she'd dated. They'd gotten the scare of their lives once they'd met her family.

When her phone rang, she looked at the caller ID and was relieved to see it was Nina and not her mother.

"Yo."

"Articulate. All of that money on a college education and that's the best you can do? What am I going to do with you?" Nina said this dryly and it made Tracy laugh.

"What do you want, old woman?"

"Hmpf! Well, I was calling to warn you that we've just had a visit from a certain furry mother-in-law who mentioned stopping by your place, but if you have that attitude…"

"Crap!"

"Yes. Well. I hear that there's a nice werewolf boy who'd love to take you to dinner at Canlis and woo you. Because, you know, if I'm not going to breed a few puppies for her for a few years, you have to."

"Milton and I are on our way."

"Bring a bag and stay over."

Tracy grinned. "Okay, twist my arm. Thanks, old woman."

"You're welcome, dog girl."

She hung up and slid into her sneakers. Quickly, she tossed her dirty dishes into the dishwasher before running to toss some clothes into a bag.

Going to the door, she whistled. "Milton? Let's hit it. Wanna go for a ride over to Auntie Nina's?"

Hearing Nina's name, Milton barked and ran to wait by the front door, tail wagging gaily. Nina was as goofy as the dog and they got along famously.

She finally let out a relieved breath as they drove away from the house. She really had to deal with this situation with her mother or consider transferring Packs to keep from going insane.

* * * * *

Gabe Murphy looked at the contents of his suitcases and double-checked the orderly placement of shoes and underwear. His personal assistant was very good about such things. Because he traveled so often she knew exactly what he wanted and how he liked it. She called and checked on weather, made his hotel reservations and set up his meeting space. All the benefits of a wife without the responsibilities.

Looking at himself in the mirror above his dresser, he smoothed down his tie, tucked his shirt into his pants and ran fingers down his pleats. The man looking back at him had a small bit of salt-and-pepper at the temples of the caramel-brown hair. Deep brown eyes gazed back at him, fringed by sooty black lashes. He was tall even for a werewolf. But he hadn't started off as a wolf anyway. He had been changed while a graduate student at Harvard nearly twenty years before. The wolf that attacked him was the son of a very prominent member in the National Pack. And when that wolf had visited him in the hospital it was with an offer to rise in the ranks of the National Pack structure in exchange for excellent grades, superior service to the Clan and his silence to the police, Gabe weighed his massive student loan debt, his lack of family connection and the chance at a high-paying job and a limitless future based on his performance and he jumped at the opportunity.

And he had risen. That wolf had become a father figure to him who taught him everything he knew about mediating. Through Harvard Law, the Pack had paid the bills and he'd learned. Three years before he'd stepped into the Mediator spot and loved every moment of it.

Usually he'd set up mediations in a third-party territory. The problem in this case was that the nearest Clan spaces were in Canada or California. In the end, he'd decided to hold meetings in Pacific's territory. He chose Portland for a number of reasons, foremost was the relative power of Cascadia Clan. They were one of the most powerful Packs in the United States and far more powerful than Pacific. To level the playing field a bit, he wanted Lex Warden out of his comfort zone.

Border disputes between Packs weren't uncommon at all. In this case, with Portland being the seat of Pacific governance, being so close to the border with Washington and Cascadia territory, things tended to bleed into each other. Most of the problems were with Cascadia wolves who worked and lived on the border of the territory. A simple expansion of a buffer zone should work to diffuse most of the tension.

He did hate to leave right at that moment though. Trouble was brewing. He'd fielded several calls already that month from different National Pack members. Many were concerned about Warren Pellini's hold on the vice president and various members of his staff. Truth was, Gabe was concerned about it too, and had quietly spoken to the Alpha about it. At the moment it was all he could do, and he didn't want to be accused of plotting against the Second, so he would think on it while he was on the West Coast.

He read through the file on his way to the airport. He'd heard a lot about the Wardens and the Lawrences and was impressed with both Pacific and Cascadia. There'd been a bit of trouble some eighteen months before when a human had been attacked at the Cascadia Pack house and had managed to defeat their Third, who'd turned up dead with the Pellini Family written all over it.

Gabe frowned. He disliked Warren Pellini intensely. The man was a toad and very bad for the image of werewolves. If the humans ever got wind of the very idea of a werewolf mafia it would set interspecies relations back decades.

* * * * *

Tracy bounded up the stairs from the garage and Milton blew past her and straight to where Nina was standing in the kitchen.

"Stinky!" Nina grinned and knelt down and hugged the dog. Straightening, she tossed him a chunk of cheese and tipped her chin at Tracy. "Yo, Stinky's mom, what's up?"

"I'll just go put this in the guest room." Tracy held up the bag. "Don't steal my dog and don't feed him tofu dogs, blech!"

"They're tofu *corn* dogs and he loves them." Milton barked to underline his love of the tiny corn dogs.

Cade wandered into the kitchen, distaste clear on his face. "Bad enough she's got a three-legged dog, you're feeding him those nasty things?"

"Shut up, fur butt. He's just fine. Your steaks are on the grill as we speak so you don't have to sully your oh-so-manly stomach with tofu pups."

"Werewolves are not tofu eaters," Lex said as he came into the room.

"Is that from the official how-to manual?" Nina raised her eyebrow at him. "And he's not a werewolf, he's a dog. I know there's not a huge difference and you both have that blank, slightly dazed look around food, but still."

Tracy snickered as she came into the kitchen and kissed Nina's cheek. "Thanks for the heads-up. Close call."

"She's just trying to help. She wants you to be happy." Cade drank a beer and checked the steaks on the large indoor grill.

"Yeah and isn't it nice she hounds me instead of you?" Tracy dug in the fridge and pulled out a beer of her own.

"Well, that is a bonus. I've tried to put her on Nina and Lex. If they gave her grandchildren she'd really back off." Cade grinned at Nina, who threw a potholder at his head.

"If you think I'm going to breed a litter because your mother can't join the garden club or whatever other women her age do instead of harassing her children, you're all nuts. Lex and I will have children on our schedule. I would have been in a bigger hurry if you people hadn't made me a werewolf. Now that I know I have nearly double the lifespan, I'm good. Anyway, I don't know if I like the Pack enough to bring a child into it."

Nina was still hurting that the Pack had stood by as she was attacked and nearly killed. It was her mission to make them all more democratic and a heck of a lot less bigoted toward humans. It was a sore spot and she didn't want to have children who would be part of that hierarchy until she could feel better about it.

The room got quiet for a moment. It was an old argument. Lex got up and kissed the top of Nina's head and hugged her, not knowing what else to do. He loved her and she was his and he kept hoping the situation would mellow over time.

"So when does the big bad Mediator come to town?" Tracy asked to change the subject. "This whole thing reminds me of the scene in *La Femme Nikita* when they bring in the Cleaner and everyone gets all freaked out and scared."

"Ah, I was meaning to talk to you about that. He's holding the mediations in Portland. You want to come down and help me? Nina is coming, and well, we all know how very good she is at holding her tongue and playing werewolf politics. I'd like your help in managing the paperwork. Nina, tongue firmly held," Lex looked at his wife with narrowed eyes and she shrugged and tossed Milton a corn dog with a bit of mustard, "will be my eyes. She's good at knowing when people are up to something. But I'd like someone who can help with the Pack politics. Cade will stay here but I get to bring three wolves and I'd like it to be you, Nina and Megan."

"How come he's not coming here?"

Cade plated up the steaks and carried them to the table, where they all went to sit down. Milton went to lie in the corner near the fireplace on his dog bed, sated with the food Nina had given him.

"He's a mediator. He's going to come in, tell Nick and me that we're both full of shit, kick our asses and make us each give up something and work to find a solution. If he had it here, he'd be giving me a lot of power. Ours is the more powerful Pack by far. I get it. But I think it'll be a relatively quick process too. We get along well with Pacific and it's not a big deal to enlarge the buffer."

"So why is Nina coming? I mean, no offense, I think traveling with Nina is a hoot and all. But if it's a quick thing and you can trust the Lawrences and this mediator, why have her sneaky-peeky eyes on them?"

Nina snorted. "A hoot? You go with that big vocabulary, teen wolf." Tracy made a score mark in the air with a finger. "Anyway, my theory is that he doesn't trust me to be here without him."

"He's afraid I'll steal her away." Cade smirked and Nina laughed.

"Dream on. Is it a crime to want to be with my mate and take advantage of hotel sex?"

Tracy put her hands up in surrender. "Ugh! That's enough sharing, thanks. So okay, well, yes. I'm sure I can get Charity to deal with the store for a few days. When do we go?"

"Tomorrow, if you can work it."

"Let me call her and see. You know we have to stay in a place where I can have Milton."

Lex looked at the dog, who was now on his back, three legs in the air, tongue lolling out the side of his mouth. "That dog isn't firing on all cylinders."

Nina smacked his arm. "Hey! He enjoys life. He's a Lab, they're all a bit goofy but he's very smart, you know. You just underestimate him. You do that a lot for someone who is supposedly the Big Bad Enforcer. Take one look and dismiss."

He grinned and kissed her hard. "You're right, beautiful. I'm sure Milton is a genius. You were certainly a wolf in sheep's clothing. Or a siren in librarian's clothing."

"You're so going to get lucky."

"Ugh. I'm going to go call Charity." Tracy pushed away from the table and went into the office.

They finished dinner and Lex went to make calls while Nina and Cade cleaned up the kitchen.

"You'll take care of him, right?" Cade asked quietly as the two worked side by side. "And Tracy too?"

She quirked up a smile and gave him a soft kiss on the lips. "Of course. Nobody is going to fuck them over on my watch. I promise."

His hand stayed at her hip, thumb sliding back and forth over the exposed skin between her sweater and pants. Her heart sped up as it always did when he turned his attention on her like that.

Their connection through the tri-bond tied them together emotionally and physically, and because Cade and Lex were brothers, in many ways Nina was biologically close to being his mate too.

"I'm going to miss your smart mouth," he murmured and stepped back before he did something monumentally stupid like lean in and kiss her.

She smiled, a bit of bittersweetness at the edges. There was so much there between them that would never be realized. Despite that, other than Lex, he was her heart and she loved him as a friend and brother and as her Alpha, and a part that she tucked away loved him as a man. But she would never let that part free because Lex was her everything. He was what made her take every breath, her laughter and her annoyance and her safety and comfort. He was her other half.

"I'll call you every day and bitch at you. I have a list, you know."

He barked out a surprised laugh and turned on the dishwasher. "I bet you do. You call me if things get out of hand."

She nodded and shrugged. She wouldn't call without Lex's input. Cade was her Alpha, yes, but she didn't follow him blindly and she wouldn't go around Lex, especially when it concerned his job. Nina knew that Cade didn't mean it in that way, he just cared deeply about his siblings and his wolves, but it was not something she'd do.

"I'm going to go and Pack. Lex is hopeless at it. Good night." She put a hand up and pushed the hair out of his eyes and turned and left the room.

Cade leaned back against the counter and sighed, scrubbing his hands over his face. He knew she was not his. He'd never betray his brother, Nina or his Pack that way but god he wanted her.

"Hey." Tracy walked into the room.

Cade looked around his hands at his youngest sister. She hopped up on the counter and looked at him, seeing it all. "Did you get things arranged at your store?"

"Yeah, Charity is going to handle it. You okay?"

He tousled those golden curls and cupped her cheek. "Yeah. I'm fine. You…I…Nina and I…"

"I know. Neither of you ever would. Lex knows that too. It's hard with brothers sharing the tri-bond. Layla has feelings for her anchor too. It's a common enough thing. You'll find your own mate and it'll be easier."

"I hope so. I'd like to find her. What about you?"

"Yeah, I'd like to find him. I want to share my life with someone and as an added bonus, Mom would have to move on to you, Megan and Tegan."

He rolled his eyes. "Lucky me. Now go to bed. You're all going to be getting on the road pretty early in the morning."

She jumped down and he hugged her. "'Night, Cade. I love you."

"I love you too." He kissed her forehead. "Eyebrow ring." He shuddered and she laughed and turned and left the room, that dog of hers following in her wake.

Chapter Two

ဢ

Nick Lawrence rolled out of his bed at six-thirty and stretched. He needed to get a workout in before he went out to meet with the Mediator and the Wardens at ten.

He jumped in the shower and put on jeans and a sweater before going back into the bedroom. Opening the curtains, the room brightened.

He sauntered back toward the bed. "Shelley, you need to wake up," he leaned over and whispered to the redhead currently curled up in his bed.

She woke up and smiled. "Again?"

Laughing, he straightened. "As good an offer as that is, I need to get out the door. The Mediator is in town and I need to prepare. I'll drop you at home on my way to the gym."

She sighed and stretched to entice him. He thought about it for a few moments but pushed it away. He didn't have time. He wanted to work out to clear his head.

Seeing that he was set on what he had to do, she swung her very long legs out of bed and padded into the bathroom. He knew she'd hurry it up. She wasn't prone to playing games or being difficult. It was one of the reasons he liked her and took her out from time to time.

Nick liked his life. He was thirty years old and second in a Pack with excellent territory. Like the Wardens, his family had dominated the Pack leadership for nearly two hundred years. His brother was Alpha and Nick was fine with that. His brother had a mate and two kids, the future of the Pack was assured and that gave him the freedom to play.

At the gym, he did his Krav Maga workout and some boxing before a good swim, all the while working through the issues in his head. Nick didn't actually think it was a problem. He liked Lex Warden and thought the Cascadia Pack was fair for a much, much larger and more powerful neighbor. It could have been way worse.

At the same time, two Enforcers from different Packs in the same room would be a huge hassle and he knew it. He could feel his wolf pushing at him, competitive and raging to defeat a perceived challenger.

It was a good thing the Mediator would be there. He'd be much higher in rank than either one of them, even though he was Third in his own Pack. The National Pack was made up of the most powerful wolves in the nation and as such, the Mediator would be more powerful than even an Alpha of another territory.

Showering, he put on a suit and tie and headed to the Pack house to speak with Ben and to pick up his personal assistant.

He smiled as he pulled his Porsche into the driveway. The house was the one he grew up in. His parents still lived on the grounds in a house they'd built after handing Pacific over to Ben fifteen years before, when Nick was still a teenager. The main house was a very large Victorian with big trees all around, a big wraparound porch and even a tire swing in the side yard next to Ben's kids' huge playset.

"Whoo-hoo! Don't you clean up nice." Ben Lawrence looked up at his brother when he entered the room.

"I get by. You got anything else for me? We're set to meet in an hour."

The Mediator had chosen a resort-type hotel outside the city that had expansive grounds. The meeting space would be much different there than if he'd chosen a downtown hotel. More relaxed than corporate.

"You can do your job just fine. I spoke briefly with Cade earlier today. I trust you, I trust them. But I would like you to feel them out on the whole Pellini mess."

"Gotcha. I'm curious myself but guessing that they aren't happy with it. There was that mess with their demoted Third turning up dead and it looked like a family hit. Can't imagine that engendered much positive feeling between them and Cascadia."

"Yeah. Well, we don't want to go getting in the middle of this situation, Nick. The Pellinis are powerful. Who knows? Maybe when this is over they'll remember that we didn't take sides."

"I'm not sure it's wise to not take sides. This is the mafia, Ben! They'll bring us all down if we let them."

"Just feel them out for now, Nick." Ben frowned for a moment and relaxed. "Nina Warden and the youngest sister will be there along with Lex and one of the guards for Nina. How many people are you taking?"

"I'll take one of my men as backup. I have no doubt that the Mediator will have a full retinue of guards and I'm not fooled by how hot Nina Warden is. She'd rip my throat out as soon as look at me if I threatened hers. I haven't met the youngest sister, is she a guard too?"

"No. Not the youngest one. Cade says she's just administrative help and he didn't sound like he was hiding anything. If she's female, I'm guessing you'll charm her. But don't screw this one, Nick. The last thing we need are two angry Wardens down here ready to kill the wolf who hurt their baby sister."

Nick shrugged. "Like I can help it. But you know, I do have control over my cock, thank you very much. Sheesh." He grinned at his brother, who snorted. "I'm off. I want to grab some coffee before I get there."

He saw his personal assistant and one of his guards in the hall and they all headed out.

* * * * *

"I can't believe you made us get up at five." Tracy held on to her latte like it was her lifeline as they drove up the winding drive to the resort.

Nina laughed. "He said early. And you slept for most of the way here."

"I had to keep my eyes closed to keep from seeing you maul each other. Jeez. The honeymoon is over. I thought you weren't so hot for each other after the first six months."

"I've got news for you, sweetie, this mate thing is like sexual crack. I think I know why your mom was so unhappy all those years. Your dad was gone so much, she must have gone up the walls. Not being around Lex for long periods of time makes me very unhappy and when I'm with him I just want to touch him, nuzzle and snuggle with him. It's irresistible."

"Blech! So I'll be all horny like you two are all the time?"

Lex chuckled. "Is being horny a bad thing?"

"I suppose not if you have a mate to satisfy your urges. But really, do you have to do it in front of me and Megan?"

"Jealous?" Nina smirked at Tracy over her shoulder and laughed.

"I am!" Megan said and patted Milton's head.

"Wow, this is some place," Tracy said as they pulled up to the main building. The drive had taken them up a hill into dense foliage. The grounds were landscaped in a lush manner so that even though it was full winter, it was still green.

There were some lovely water features and what looked to be a hedge maze that Tracy thought she'd take a look at later on.

The main building was done in the Craftsman style of architecture, dominating the grounds with its natural wood beams, and beautiful stained glass in the windows. Tracy loved the signature style, it felt very indicative of the spirit of the Northwest. She saw that there were many small outbuildings in the same style grouped all over the grounds.

"I'm going to check us all in, I'll be right back," Lex said and leaned over and kissed Nina. "Stay out of trouble. Megan, shoot her if she looks like she's going to get out."

Nina sighed and flicked his ear.

Once he'd walked into the building, she turned to look at her sisters-in-law in the backseat. "So, let's take Milton for a walk."

"No. We'll wait. Come on, he's going to have a stroooohh..." Megan's eyes glazed over. The other two women followed her gaze and saw the men getting out of the cars just over from where they were parked.

"Holy hot studly dude," Nina breathed as she watched the man in the dark suit get out of the Porsche. "Correction, holy hot studly wolf. That's Nick Lawrence. I met him briefly when Lex and I were on our road trip down to San Francisco this last summer."

"I'm all sweaty all of a sudden. And we have to sit in a room with him for a day or so? Whew, that'll be a treat. Maybe we should make up stuff to have to mediate. I bet he's cute when he's mad." Tracy snickered.

"The others with him aren't so bad either," Megan murmured, checking out the other wolf she guessed was a guard and one who looked like a sexy accountant. "Man, I need to get laid."

Nina laughed, surprised. "Well, well, well! All three of them certainly look like prime mattress material. Go for it, Megs."

Lex walked out of the building and stopped when he saw Nick. Back in the car, the women watched as they talked for a few moments.

"Ugh, I feel like the little woman sitting out here in the car! Gah! Well, at least Lawrence walks like a man with not much to hide. He's a ladies' man though."

"How can you tell? Jeez, you can't be that good." Tracy leaned forward between the seats.

"He has a cocky walk. A loose, self-confident walk. He's extraordinarily good-looking and well-groomed. He's got the chick magnet sports car. It only stands to reason. Plus, he's the second son. He has the freedom that the oldest one wouldn't have had. Look at the difference between Cade and Lex. Don't think I don't know what Lex was like before he sniffed me."

Lex walked back to the car and looked suspicious when they all got quiet but for stifled giggles when he got inside. "What is going on?"

"Nothing. I was just saying that Nick Lawrence was a ladies' man and explaining how I knew. Get us checked in all right?"

Lex narrowed his eyes at her and then handed her a map. "We're around the corner in a bungalow. The dog will have space and Megan can be nearby to keep an eye on you."

Nina smiled. She loved how sweet he was under that tough wolf exterior. "Thank you, Scooby. We should get our crap unloaded then. It's coming up on the meeting time."

He pulled the car around and they moved the stuff into the bungalow, fed and watered Milton and let him do a quick run.

"Go on, I'll be up in a second," Tracy called out. "I just want to let him run a bit more before I go."

"You know where it's at then?"

"Yes, Lex. You showed us on the map four times already. And I won't be late, I promise. And no, I'm not going to change. It's stupid. He's going to mediate a buffer and I don't need pantyhose for that."

Nina shoved Lex up the walk and Megan waved back at Tracy and then moved to flank Nina.

Tracy let Milton run a few minutes more and took him back inside, made sure it was warm enough, gave him a treat and opened up the drapes so he could look outside. He liked to watch the birds and squirrels. Taking one last look in the mirror, she headed out to the conference room where they'd be meeting.

It was a nice day, crisp but unseasonably warm, and she only needed a light jacket over her T-shirt as she walked along the path. Her heart caught in her throat as she watched a man with caramel hair and a bit of salt-and-pepper at the temples walk into the building in front of her. He had on pants with a pleat so sharp it probably cut paper, expensive shoes and a wine-colored sweater. The perfect mix of formal and casual to go with the perfect haircut. Very attractive in a professorial way. Still, she had the urge to jump on him and muss him up.

The man was in charge. His very demeanor indicated he was self-assured and oh-so-very dominant. Mmm, dominant.

She laughed to herself and went in behind the man, who was quite obviously the Mediator. There was a coat rack just outside the room and she took off hers and hung it up. The room was warm enough for humans and definitely warm enough for wolves. She couldn't resist a quick look in the window to catch her reflection. Her lipstick was still on nicely and she gave her hair a quick fingercomb and went into the room.

Nick looked up from the paperwork on the table in front of him and caught sight of the woman that had just entered the room. Shoulder-length, tousled golden-blonde curls framed her face. The sweet heart shape and pixie nose were set off by the ring in her eyebrow. Freckles dusted her cheeks and drew his eyes up past her high cheekbones to the green eyes. They were wide and glittering with hidden mischief. Her lips, stained red with shiny gloss, curved up on one corner like she had a secret.

She reached up and tucked her hair back and more piercings, running the length of her ear, showed. When she turned and waved to Lex he could see the outline of both nipples, each pierced by a ring, through the tight black T-shirt she had on. Her features seemed petite but she was long and lithe and sexy. Her legs were very nice legs, showcased by the worn and faded jeans she was wearing, but her ass was spectacular.

He should be horrified. He should be mentally sneering and looking for the woman in the Jones New York suit and the two-hundred-dollar haircut. Instead, he stood openmouthed and panting over a woman who he wouldn't pick up hitchhiking.

Tracy nonchalantly looked for the Mediator while pretending to be all business. Waving to Lex and Nina, she did a quick sweep of the room and stopped when she saw Nick Lawrence close up.

Everything got still and quiet as her eyes were drawn to the sable black hair that she just knew was cut to perfection every six weeks. It looked soft and silky and she clenched her hands at the thought of running her fingers through it. His eyes caught hers and pulled her into their deep blue depths. His features were beautiful, almost pretty, and yet the width of his shoulders and the power hinted at in his legs overcame it. It was clear he was a man. A big, bad man who could be scary if he needed to be. He wouldn't be the Enforcer if he wasn't physically the strongest and most fearsome wolf in the Pack.

She shivered. And then felt confused. Why on earth did that matter? She'd never been one to go after the jock type and most especially the clean-cut, corporate-suit type.

"Tracy? You ready to get started?" Lex asked, jolting her out of her thoughts.

"Uh, yes. Yes. Sorry." She walked over to their table and sat next to him. Behind them both, Nina watched with a puzzled look on her face.

Professor Studly stepped forward and everyone stood again. "I'm Gabe Murphy, the Mediator for the National Pack. This doesn't appear to be an overly complicated situation so I'm hoping we can cut the shit and get this thing banged out by the end of business today."

He held out his hand to Lex, who shook it.

"I'm Alexander Warden, Lex to most people. I'm Enforcer and Second in the Cascadia Clan." He inclined his head slightly, showing the deference due the Mediator but not an inch more.

"It's a pleasure to meet you, Lex. I've heard a lot about you."

Gabe stepped to Nick then, who was still staring at Tracy, but forced himself to focus on the Mediator. "Nicholas Lawrence, Enforcer and Second in Pacific Clan." He too gave the inclination of his head.

Acting by strict protocol, Gabe moved back to Lex, where Nina stood forward. "Nina Reyes–Warden. Second."

Gabe couldn't help but grin. The woman clearly thought the whole thing was bullshit. It showed in her body language and the way she met his eyes. He liked that. "I've also heard about you, Nina. It's nice to finally meet you, your reputation proceeds you."

She snorted. Lex looked horrified and Tracy and Megan kept their gazes down so as not to laugh.

"I'll take that as a compliment then, shall I, Gabe?"

He laughed then. "Absolutely."

He then dealt with the other members of each group. Despite his normally calm demeanor, his heart sped up when he shook the hand of Tracy Warden. Normally he'd have been none too thrilled to meet someone with a facial piercing, at the very least turned off, but on her it was wicked sexy. Made him wonder if anything else was pierced, and if she had tattoos.

"Okay, do you all know each other?" Gabe asked, looking around at them, forcing his mind off stripping those clothes off Tracy Warden and searching out the answers to his questions.

"I've not met anyone from Pacific." Tracy was surprised that her voice didn't crack under the pressure of all that testosterone in the room.

Gabe took her hand, led her over to the others and introduced her to Nick. When Nick touched her hand her body tightened and erupted into gooseflesh. *Oh shit.*

"It's a pleasure to meet you, Tracy." Nick said this in his usual debonair way but he was fighting down panic. Fighting back the urge to push her back to the table behind her and grab the flesh of her neck between his teeth.

She knew she must have mumbled something and met the others. She realized this as she sat in the chair next to Lex and began to take notes. The time began to tick by and she didn't quite know where it had gone.

The feel of her hand in Nick's had warmed her. Turned her insides molten. She was achy and her wolf was agitated. Several times Lex had to repeat himself when he asked her a question as she found it increasingly more difficult to pay attention.

Nina watched her sister-in-law with careful eyes. All the fidgeting and distractedness was unlike her. "Excuse me, can we take a break?" Nina asked, standing up.

Lex turned around, concern on his face. "Are you all right?"

"I just need a break. I think I need a piece of fruit or something."

"Of course, we've been at this for a few hours. Let's take half an hour and then we'll work through lunch. I took the liberty of ordering in, I hope you don't mind." Gabe stood, smiling.

Nina nodded and moved forward. "Tracy, honey, can you come with me, please?" And before Tracy could answer she found herself being dragged out of the room.

Just outside the building, Nina hustled her around the side. "What the hell is going on? Are you all right?" Nina examined her through narrowed eyes.

"Wha—what do you mean?"

Nina rolled her eyes. "If you don't tell me, I'll just tell Lex and then it'll be all dramatic. I've been watching you, Trace. You're the attention-to-details queen and for the last two hours you've been mooning—and yes, I said mooning—over Nick Lawrence and he's been just as bad."

Tracy put her head in her hands, unable to deny it. "Oh god, Nina. I think he's my mate!"

"What? Are you kidding me?"

"Do you think I'd kid about something like this? I've never been affected by a male like this before. I want to rub my face all over him. I want to give him my neck. I want him!"

"Nina! Where the hell are you?" Lex yelled from the doors around the corner.

"I'm back here. Go get me some fruit and a bagel or something, please."

He came around the corner, emanating menace. "What is going on, Nina? Are you all right?"

Nina sighed and patted his arm. "I'm fine. Thank you, baby. Now, please, I need to talk to Tracy alone. Can you please get me something to eat?"

"Are you pregnant?"

She stared at him, mouth agape and then burst out laughing. "No, studly. I'm not. I promise. This is female-type stuff, though, so I'd appreciate the privacy."

Thinking that he may be sent off to retrieve tampons or something equally horrifying, he set Megan on watch and headed to get some food.

Nina giggled and turned back to Tracy as Megan hustled over to them. "He thought I was going to send him for feminine hygiene products or something. I'm going to have to keep that reaction in mind for the future. Now, back to you."

"What am I going to do?"

"What do you mean? If he's your mate, there's only one thing you can do!"

"Mate? What the hell did I miss?" Megan hissed.

"Tracy is pretty sure that Nick is her mate," Nina explained in low tones.

Megan's eyebrow went up. "Well, nice one! He's a hot number."

Tracy's misery was chased away when she had to laugh at her sister. "He's from another Pack."

"And?"

"I'd always imagined my mate to be from Cascadia."

"Yes well, I'd always imagined my mate to be a human man with a normal job who didn't turn into a wolf at will and carry a gun. We don't always get what we think we want." Nina's face softened. "But a lot of the time we get what we need."

"Just get a good sniff and let him get one too. Nature will take over from there, Trace." Megan's matter-of-factness was a comfort and Tracy snorted.

"I need some time alone," Tracy said with a sigh. "I need some fresh air and time to think. We've got fifteen minutes left. I'll be back."

"Are you sure?" Nina looked concerned.

"Yeah. Thanks."

Nina hugged her and Megan followed. "I'm happy for you, Tracy. This is a good thing, you know," Megan murmured into her ear.

"I hope so."

They walked back into the building and Tracy headed down the path and ended up at the hedge maze. She wandered down the first wide lane and headed left, toward a bench near a fountain.

Sitting down, she put her head back and looked up at the sky.

That's how Nick found her. When she'd left with the others, he'd tried to talk himself into staying in the room. Tried to pretend that what he was feeling was just raw lust but had failed. His wolf had chafed at that and pushed him into getting up and out of the room and he'd followed her scent on the wind.

"Hi," he said as he approached the bench.

She sat up slowly, her eyes meeting his, and everything else simply ceased to exist. "Hi."

Dropping onto the bench beside her, he couldn't resist any longer. "I need to know." He leaned in, put his face into her neck and breathed in deeply.

It hit him then—her pheromones slamming into his system, twining with his senses, luring him, seducing him. Her scent called to him, her chemicals tangoed with his and he groaned, his entire body hardening with want for her. Not just physical desire but the need to possess her in every way.

He clenched his fists to keep from ripping her clothes off.

"Oh," she said faintly when he moved his head back, keeping his face close to her own. His eyes locked on her lips, red and shiny, and his breath caught when she licked them nervously.

He forced himself to stay still when she leaned in and breathed deeply of him, but it was too much when he watched her physical reaction, saw the gooseflesh work up the back of her neck. When he could smell her body blooming for him, scent her desire creamy between her thighs. He groaned again and put a hand to her chin, moving her face back so he could see into her eyes.

"Tracy?"

She nodded, wordless and he moved so that their lips touched and the flames jumped and consumed them both. One of his arms banded around her waist and pulled her to him tightly as his mouth devoured hers.

His tongue was hot and wet as it slid against her teeth and into her mouth. The dance of movement between them was all-encompassing. There was nothing but strained breathing and soft sighs.

"God, I have to have you," Nick said as his mouth moved to her jaw.

"Yes, oh yes." She scrambled into his lap, straddling him, and he pulled her jacket off and then her shirt and stilled for a moment when he saw her breasts. They were small and perky and she had the loveliest pink nipples. Even the rings piercing each one worked on him. She arched her back, grinding herself into him, and they both moaned at the contact with his cock.

"Off, off, off!" she murmured as her hands worked at his belt and the button and zipper of his fly. Suddenly his cock was free and in her hands and the pleasure of that contact was so good as it rushed through him that it made him slightly faint. He'd had a lot of sex with a lot of sexy women but even while buried deep in the hottest of them he'd never felt as totally electrified by pleasure as he did with his cock in her hand.

He groaned and pulled at her jeans, opening them and standing her up long enough to work them down her thighs. It took a moment more of frustrated work to get her boot off and one leg of the jeans free and she was back on his lap, naked against his clothed body, and he was so turned on that when she brushed herself over his cock he shuddered with it and had to clench his teeth to keep from coming then and there.

"If you don't put yourself inside of me and right now, I'm going to fall over dead," she said.

He laughed and put a hand between her thighs, fingers brushing through the folds of her pussy to be sure she was ready. And was she ever. Swollen, hot and so juicy that his cock jumped in anticipation.

Her head fell back and he slowly drew circles around her clit with slick fingertips and took a nipple between his teeth. She arched into him with a pleading cry and rolled her hips into his hand.

"You're so beautiful," he said, lips brushing against her nipple. His fingers slid into her and his thumb came up and across her clit. She whimpered and her hands went into his hair.

The weak winter sun shone down on her skin. She should have been cold but the heat of her desire for him warmed her. There weren't even words for how much she wanted him, for how she felt at that moment. Drowning in him, needing him so much she ached with it, each touch of his mouth, of his hands on her, drove her into a frenzy. Her wolf paced inside her, recognizing his wolf, and she'd never felt so out of control and yet so very right all at once.

He bit down gently on her nipple and pressed hard on her clit with his thumb and her climax hurtled through her with blinding intensity. She had to bite her bottom lip to keep from screaming but a moan that came from deep inside her escaped anyway, and he echoed it.

"I have to fuck you, baby. Are you ready?"

"Yesyesyesyes," she whispered, body still tingling from orgasm.

She moved up on her knees and their fingers brushed against each other as she reached back to help guide him into her.

Eyes locked, she sank down on him, pulling his cock deep inside her body.

"Oh, yes. You're so fucking perfect, Tracy. Your pussy is so tight and hot."

She hummed her satisfaction with the thick girth of his cock and the words that flowed from him as she rocked against him slowly, enjoying the way he felt buried inside her.

"I can't be slow. I need this. I can't..." His words strangled as he stood and took over. She wrapped her legs around his waist, locking her ankles at the small of his back. In a few steps she was against the wall of the small enclosure the fountain resided in. The concrete was cold and rough against her back and the buckle of her belt dangling from the jeans still hanging around one ankle jingled with each thrust he made into her body. These small sensory bursts kept her from slipping away into the maelstrom of the storm of feeling this man evoked in her.

She tightened herself around him and held on to his shoulders as he bowed his head and fucked into her body deep and hard. Oh what a feeling it was to evoke such a depth of desire in a man like this! She could feel the hardness of him as he pushed into her over and over.

"Make me yours, Nick. Please. Come inside of me," she murmured and he groaned in response as his entire body tightened up.

"You are mine," he said in a harsh whisper just as he made one final thrust up into her and came.

With each burst of his climax, his semen filled her. He marked her and the bond began to form between them with such intensity that his knees buckled and he sank to the ground as he continued to come.

The threads of connection were there, glimmering and strong, and she felt his heart beating as if it were her own. Felt the intensity of his feelings for her. Love. Yes, love, and she felt it too.

Things were a shaky for a bit as the release of his seed worked its magic, but after a few minutes he looked up into her face.

"Wow." He kissed her chin. "Oh baby, you've got to be cold." He stood and she put her pants back on and then he handed her the shirt and jacket.

"Thanks." She pulled the shirt and jacket on and her skin missed his touch even as it warmed with clothing on. He bent, tied her boot and straightened, putting himself back into his pants.

She laughed, fixing his tie.

"Well, this will be an interesting story to tell our grandchildren someday." He frowned. "Okay well, not all of it is suitable for telling. You know what I mean."

"You're okay with this? The suddenness? I mean, I can feel your hesitancy." Which made her feel no small amount off balance and insecure.

He turned to her and pulled her close. "You're my mate. You're my everything. I'm not hesitant exactly, but more caught off-guard. This morning I had not expected to meet my mate today, you know? But I am happy and I plan to enjoy getting to know you. There are things we'll have to iron out, surely, but we can do it. We have to. And wow, I just fucked you outside in a garden. Not very romantic. I'm sorry, I just couldn't wait."

She laughed. "I couldn't wait either. I'm glad you didn't."

They walked hand in hand back to the conference room. Once inside, Lex stood up and started to yell at her for being late but everyone froze, the room full of wolves scenting the air. The evidence of their bond hung heavy and spicy around them.

"Tracy? Honey, is everything all right?" Lex stood, feeling, well, not quite sure what. Happy yes, but also slightly sad because she was now firmly someone else's and his baby sister was mated.

She smiled and nodded and he went to her, hugging her tight as they both laughed. "I'm great."

Nina stood back, grinning at them both, and then looked at Megan, who also looked happy but just a little sad around the edges.

There were collective hugs and congratulations around the room and Gabe beamed at them both. "Congratulations to both of you."

"Let's get back to work so we can finish this. I'd like to take my mate home to meet my brother and sister-in-law," Nick said.

"I've got to call Cade," Lex said.

Nina put a hand on his shoulder and leaned in, kissing his temple. "You guys get back to work, I'll call Cade."

She took her cell phone out into the alcove and dialed home.

"Hey there. Is everything okay?" Cade said as he answered the phone.

"Better than okay. Cade, Tracy found her mate."

"She what? How? Who? Jeez, you've only been down there for half a day!"

"It's Nick Lawrence and they've sealed the bond. I don't know where nor do I wish to contemplate it. But she looks very happy and so does he."

Cade sighed. "Well, oh, good."

"What is it?" Nina heard his hesitation and the sadness just behind the words.

"She'll be moving to Portland now. She'll be in another Pack. I'll miss her."

"Yeah. Me too. But Portland isn't that far, it's only three hours away. And she looks so good with him. She's glowing with it." She ached, wanting to reach out and hug him, comfort him.

"I'll contact my parents and we'll come down after details are worked out."

"He hasn't told his brother yet. Wait a while before you contact Ben."

"Okay. *Oh shit.*"

"What?"

"Tri-bond. She'll need the tri-bond and it has to be someone related to him or above him in Pack hierarchy. Ben can't because he's already mated."

"Oh! Well, maybe there's a cousin or something." Her stomach fluttered low when she remembered her own bond experience, remembered Cade's cock deep inside her.

"Maybe. I don't know them well enough to know for sure. Have her call me when she can but until then, please tell her that I'm happy for her and that I love her."

"You got it. Are you going to be all right?"

He paused for a long moment. "Yes. Thanks for asking, beautiful."

"Anytime. Cade?"

"Yeah?"

"I love you. It'll all be okay."

He sighed. "I love you too." And hung up.

The rest of the negotiations went by rather quickly. Gabe kept an iron grip on the proceedings and hammered out a deal to enlarge the buffer between the two Packs that worked for both and capitalized on the goodwill between Pacific and Cascadia.

While at the table, Tracy kept up her place as a member of the Cascadia Pack. She'd continue to do so until she officially joined Pacific. She didn't feel pressured to do anything else. Her heart would always be with Cascadia, it was the Pack of her birth and her family ruled it. She'd join Pacific because that's where Nick held position as Second and she'd give them her loyalty.

By two the papers had been signed and agreed to.

Lex stood and shook hands with Nick. He smiled at his sister. "I know you two are anxious to go to the Pacific Pack house. Would you like Milton to stay with us while you do that?" He turned to Nick. "Of course, with permission, we'll stay here and Cade and Mom and Dad will join us for the joining ceremony."

Tracy realized then just how much her life had changed in just a few hours. Everything had changed. It wasn't that she was unhappy. Quite the opposite. For wolves, finding a mate was the moment they looked forward to. Her connection to Nick filled her up and brought her joy and satisfaction in ways she hadn't even known were possible. But she'd have to build a new life and a new home with Nick.

"Joining ceremony?" Nina looked confused.

Tracy squeezed her sister-in-law's hand. "Now that Nick and I have bonded, I'll become a member of Pacific. I'll be taken into the clan and given status as Second." The look of sadness, brief before Nina smiled to cover it, made Tracy feel better.

"Of course you have permission to stay. Who is Milton?" Nick couldn't stop himself from touching Tracy. His fingers traced through her hair and she leaned into his touch.

Tracy laughed. "Milton is my dog. He's a lab and a real sweetie. I have to tell you that he comes with me everywhere."

Nick winced as he thought of his expensive apartment and the furnishings. "I don't think my building allows pets."

"Well, we'll be moving, won't we?" She said it with a raised brow and annoyance flashed through him.

"We'll have to figure it out. I mean, my apartment is so nice and it has a great view and…"

"Okay, this is something we should work out in private," Tracy cut him off, seeing Lex's agitation out of the corner of her eye. He'd begin to feel protective of her and things would be unpleasant.

"You're right, of course."

"We'll just stay here then, in the bungalow we're already in. Call us when you've got details, Tracy." Lex tried not to scowl.

Nina hesitated but went ahead and brought up the issue that had been weighing on her mind. "Uh, one thing and well, I know this probably isn't my business but as it was sort of sprung on me I think it's a serious issue — the tri-bond."

Nick stilled for a moment and Tracy blushed. "Damn. I hadn't thought about that. I'm Ben's anchor but he can't do it and I don't have any unmated male relatives."

"Well, we'll have to call someone in then."

"What? Like a personal ad? Do they have space for that in Craigslist?" Panic edged through Tracy. She knew they'd have to do the tri-bond but it hadn't quite hit her until that moment. She'd have to have sex with a stranger. As if that wasn't bad enough, they'd fly someone in? Like a pinch hitter?

The problem was that the higher up a male was in Pack hierarchy, the fewer his choices for the anchor bond. Because Nick was Second, he could only have an Alpha, or an equivalent wolf who had higher rank, or a relative. It didn't happen all the time, most wolves weren't high in Pack ranks. But it happened often enough that the National Pack kept a database of willing wolves who'd be called upon in such situations.

"What else can we do, Tracy? I'm sorry. I know this is hard on you but we can't avoid you needing the tri-bond. There's no way around that."

"I know." But she'd have to let another wolf come inside her. That seemed so intimate with a stranger. Yes, wolves didn't have to worry about STDs and she was on birth control pills, but it made her feel so uncomfortable. She supposed it was also because the anchor bond would be a part of their lives forever. He'd be an honorary member of Pacific and hold a special place of power and honor. Almost like extended family was to humans, or even as an in-law.

Gabe saw her distress and felt for her. He also outranked Nick and it certainly wouldn't be a chore to make love to Tracy. Most wolves at his rank would serve as anchors at some point and he felt like he could make that commitment to Tracy and Nick without hesitation. "Well," Gabe cleared his throat. "I'm unmated and I outrank you. If you'd be willing, I'd be honored to be Tracy's anchor."

Tracy looked to Nick and then to Gabe. Relief rushed through her. "You would? You're sure? Oh thank you!" She felt comfortable around Gabe. Perhaps it was his air of professionalism or maybe it was that he was so debonair. In any case, he may not have been someone they'd known forever but he sure wasn't a total stranger and with his position in National, he'd be on the other side of the country most of the time, which probably made it easier for Nick.

"Yes, thank you." Nick inclined his head in thanks. "Tomorrow morning? Would that work or are you on your way out of town today?"

"I'm not scheduled to fly out for two more days. Tomorrow morning would be fine."

Nick gave Gabe his address and they made arrangements to have a late breakfast and perform the bond then.

Afterwards Nick all but dragged Tracy, who agreed to have Milton stay with Nina and Lex, to his car after grabbing her small suitcase.

* * * * *

"God, if I hadn't called my brother already and he wasn't expecting us, I'd take you home and fuck you a few dozen more times. I need you, Tracy. So much that it makes it hard to think." He reached out and took her hand, twining his fingers with hers.

"Thanks for telling me that. Now I'll be thinking of little else until we do get in private."

"Good, I'd hate to be alone in this terrible achy place."

"I can't believe that less than eight hours ago, I didn't even know you and now we're married."

"I know. Twelve hours ago... Never mind, so tell me about yourself." The woman in his bed this morning seemed a million years away. All he wanted was the woman in the car with him.

She flinched. "Twelve hours ago you were with another woman." Her voice was flat.

"Yes. I won't lie to you, Tracy. There were other women. A lot of them. But that's all over now. Now there's only you."

"Well, I didn't expect you to be a virgin. We're both of age. You're a very attractive, sexy, powerful wolf with very good taste in clothes. I'm sure that got you laid. A lot."

"And did you?"

"Did I what?"

"Get laid a lot?" He was suddenly incensed at the idea of any man touching her.

"I got my share. Which is, of course, over now. Well, not the getting my share part. Just the part where I get it from anyone but you. I like sex, Nick. I like it a lot. So I hope you take vitamins and work out."

He laughed, surprised but pleased. "Do you have a boyfriend?"

"I have a husband." She gave him a grin. "And no. I did, but a few weeks ago I broke it off. I knew he wasn't my mate. He knew he wasn't. It was an exercise in futility. Plus, he didn't like Milton."

He gritted his teeth thinking about her dog. "About Milton, honey, don't you think he'd be better off with Lex and Nina? In a house where he can run? An apartment is not the place for a big dog."

"You're right. It isn't."

He smiled at her reasonable response.

"Which is why we're going to buy a house."

"I've lived in my apartment for five years. I love it!"

"You can't honestly mean to tell me that I have to give up my Pack, my city, my business and my home and you aren't willing to live in a place that accommodates my dog?"

Put that way, it did seem petty of him. But still. His apartment and its trendy furniture, the view. It was perfectly located so that he could walk to all the places he liked to go.

"We'll talk about it later. This is it," he nodded with his chin at the big house with the large tree and tire swing and the big cedar playset. The big drive was filled with cars.

"Shit. The whole damned Pack is here. I'm never going to be able to sneak you back to my…our place."

"I hope they like me."

Her voice seemed so small and unsure that he looked at her after he turned the ignition off. He touched her chin, running his thumb through the cleft there. "They'll love you. Even if for no other reason than because I do."

She took a deep breath. The moment she bonded with Nick, she took on his rank. She was Second in this clan and she had to hold her head up and own that or the other wolves would see it as weakness. She also knew that, given what he'd said on the way over and Nina's comments earlier, that there were bound to be females who'd warmed his bed there wanting to check her out and she needed to be every inch Nick's mate.

She opened the door and stepped out and he came around and shot her a look. "I was going to do that."

She grinned again. "That so?" She laughed and it shot straight to his cock. Her laugh was deep and sultry. He hadn't expected that at all. "As it happens, I can open my own door. But I'm not averse to you helping me carry stuff and kill spiders."

It was his turn to laugh as he pulled her against his body, nuzzling into her neck and breathing her in like a drug. "A tough chick werewolf like you is afraid of spiders?"

"Mmm-hmmm." Her eyes closed as she clung to him, enjoying the feel of his body against her own.

"Hey! Cut it out, we want to meet her!"

Tracy jumped back guiltily and looked up at the porch, where several people were standing.

"That's Sarah, Ben's mate," Nick said, smiling up at the tall blonde waving at them both impatiently.

"And you're her anchor."

He turned to her. "Yes. Is that going to bother you?"

"Would it matter if it did?"

He caressed the line of her jaw and drew his thumb over her bottom lip. "Of course it matters. I love you. You're my mate and your happiness is very important to me. Not that I can change being her anchor."

"I know. Thank you."

He smiled and leaned in to kiss her.

"Nick! You tease, bring the girl up here so we can welcome her into the Pack!"

Nick pulled back with a groan. "And that is Ben, my brother and the Alpha. He's…"

"Yeah, I have one too."

He held out a hand and she took it and he drew her into the yard and toward the porch, where it looked like at least a dozen people were standing.

"Oh jeez," she murmured under her breath. And damn it, did that Sarah have to be so damned beautiful? She was the feminine type, with perfect creamy skin and big china-doll eyes. Knowing how Cade felt about Nina, she wondered just how deeply Nick felt for Sarah and jealousy knifed through her.

Ben came down the porch steps with a big smile on his face, and without a word to Nick, pulled Tracy into a big hug. He kissed both of her cheeks and stepped back, looking at her and then at Nick.

"Congratulations! And welcome. Welcome to Pacific and welcome to the family, Tracy."

She couldn't help but give the man a lopsided grin. He was so not suave like Nick. He wore jeans and a Trail Blazers shirt and his hair was sort of mussed up, but not in the intentional messy way that Nick's hair was.

"Thank you. I take it you're Ben."

"Oh, yes. I'm sorry. Tracy, this is my brother, Ben Lawrence, the Alpha of Pacific Clan." Nick raised a brow as his brother stared at Tracy.

"And I'm Sarah." She came down the steps and gave Tracy an appraising look that put Tracy on edge.

"Nice to meet you, Sarah." And she hoped she meant it. She wanted to fit into this family as well as she fit into her own in Seattle. She had a new Pack now and it would be a good thing if she had even a shadow of the connection with Sarah that she had with Nina.

"It's more than nice to meet you, Tracy. I can't be more thrilled that Nick has found you." With that she leaned in and kissed Tracy's cheek and stood back, her body against Ben's. Tracy couldn't quite get rid of the unease that slid through her stomach but chalked it up to nervousness.

The next hour went by in a blur of activity and new faces. She knew which females Nick had slept with by the looks they threw her. But Nick had eyes for her and her only. Ben and Nick's parents were so happy to meet her.

"I really need to talk to my brother and my parents," Tracy murmured to Nick as the evening set in.

"Oh, of course. How long have you been up? You drove down this morning, didn't you?"

"Just before five," she said, trying not to yawn. "And I'll need to talk to Charity, she's the woman who manages my store, to arrange for some more time, and I'll have to figure out what to do with it and my house."

Just how much she was leaving behind hit him square in the face. Her family, her friends, her house, her business, her

Pack. All of that for him. A wave of tender protectiveness rose in him.

"Come on, baby, let's get you home." He stood and helped her up. "Folks, thanks for the evening but Tracy and I are going home now. We'll see you all tomorrow night for the joining."

Chris and Haley, Ben and Sarah's children, got up and latched on to Nick. "Uncle Nick! Don't go!"

He laughed and swooped both of them up into his arms, kissing them both soundly. "Got to, kiddos. Tracy is tired and it's my job to take care of her. Like how your daddy takes care of your mommy."

"Ew! You're gonna kiss on her all the time then?" Chris asked, disgusted by the very idea.

Tracy laughed. "I hope so!"

* * * * *

The drive to his apartment was quiet but relaxed. He was a little concerned that his brother had taken him aside and grilled him about whether he was sure Tracy was his true mate but they'd been friendly to her face and that was a relief. Tracy seemed far more at ease now than she had earlier as well.

"Are you feeling better now?"

"Hmm?" She stretched and his heart thudded against his rib cage. "Oh, yes. Your family is lovely." Except for the women who'd hated her on sight and the Fourth who seemed annoyed that a wolf with an eyebrow ring was suddenly ranked above him. Oh and maybe Sarah, who sort of seemed to like her, but Tracy still wondered about her connection with Nick.

He pulled into the garage of a swank high-rise and up a few levels until he pulled into a spot near the elevators and turned off the ignition.

"Come on, baby. We're home."

She bit back her response, not wanting to fight. But he was going to have to accept that they needed a house with a yard for Milton.

He grabbed his briefcase and her suitcase and guided her into the elevator lobby with a hand at the small of her back. She watched as he keyed in a number on the pad near the up button. The doors slid open and they got inside the elevator car.

He hit nineteen and leaned back against the wall.

"So," she said, turning to face him, "you think this elevator has a camera in it?"

"What? Why...oh." He raised a brow and she stepped closer.

"I've never had sex in an elevator before."

"Oh, you're sin on legs, Tracy Warden. Or Lawrence. Whatever."

She chuckled and reached out, dragging a fingernail up the prominent ridge in his pants.

The elevator dinged and the doors slid open. He sighed. "Next time."

"Oh yeah." She sauntered out and he watched her sway. She had quite a lovely ass. In fact, he couldn't wait to see her naked. To really see her. That interlude in the maze was too brief and he was so crazed with need he didn't even really get a chance to look at her.

"I'm on the right. 1905."

She waited for him at the door and he couldn't unlock it fast enough. She walked in and he slammed the lock home and dropped the bags. One corner of her mouth slowly slid up into a sexy smile.

"Bedroom is right behind you," he murmured, pushing her with his body.

When they got inside she stiffened and he did too, closing his eyes at his mistake.

"It stinks of her in here."

"I…I'm sorry. I didn't know you this morning. I didn't know you last night. I didn't know."

She sighed and looked at the big bed, sheets still rumpled, the scent of sex faint in the air. The room stank of this other woman. She inhaled again. The redhead she'd met this afternoon who seemed good-natured enough.

"The redhead."

He looked at her, surprised. And then he nodded. "It wasn't ever anything between us. Just sex."

"Oh, I feel much better now. Gee, let's fuck in a bed drenched in your come for another woman!"

"I didn't know! How can you be angry when I didn't know?"

"It doesn't have to be rational!" she yelled.

"Well, that's good, because it isn't."

Her eyebrow, the one with the ring, slowly slid up and he wished he could take the words back.

"Okay, let's just deal with this. I have clean sheets, I'll change them."

He bustled past her and went to a closet and came back, arms filled with dark blue sheets.

She wandered out of the room as he worked and he found her minutes later, staring out the windows near the fireplace.

She stared out into the night at the lights of the city and the river reflecting the moon and stars. Her skin itched with need for him, with the desire to touch and be touched by him. But her head, well, that was another story. She felt off balance. It was all happening so fast. She knew how it was, she accepted that he was her mate and most certainly she felt that way. Loved him, needed him, wanted him desperately. But at the same time, she wondered why it was she had to be the one continually giving up stuff.

"I'm sorry. This isn't how I wanted our first night together to be," he said, coming up behind her and putting his arms around her waist. "The sheets are changed, I opened the windows to air it out. I'm running a bath, would you like to join me?"

She leaned her head back against his shoulder. "Yeah. And I know. We'll get past it."

"I'm going to grab some champagne. Why don't you call your family while I get everything ready?"

She turned and looked into his eyes. He wasn't that much taller than she was, just shy of six feet, so all she had to do was ease up on her tiptoes to kiss his lips softly. "Okay. I'll be in in a few minutes."

"Phone is right there behind you." He kissed her once more and left her alone to make the call.

She didn't bother calling the house, she knew that Cade and her parents would be at the resort by now with Lex and Nina, so she called Cade's cell.

"Hey there, I was getting worried about you." Cade's voice was a comfort. "Congratulations, sweetie. I'm so pleased for you."

"Thanks, Cade." Her breath hitched and she held back tears. She was happy, finding Nick was amazing, but she still felt sad at losing her old way of life. "I met his family today and they were all very nice. The joining is tomorrow night at seven at the Pack house."

"Yeah, I worked out the visit with Ben. We'll be there. I took the liberty of bringing down some more of your clothes."

She smiled, knowing that it would have been Nina's idea. "Thanks, Cade."

"You want to talk to Mom? She's over the moon."

"Uh, yes, but not right now. I'm getting ready to, uh, that is, we're going to... I just don't want to right now." She truly would cry if she heard her mother's voice, and she didn't want to deal with that right before being with Nick.

"Gotcha," he said, laughing. "Please do not elaborate. I'll tell her you'll call tomorrow. I love you, honey. We all do and we're so proud and happy that you've found your mate."

"Thank you. I am too. He's a good man with a good family."

"I'll see you tomorrow then. I love you."

"I love you too, Cade." Smiling, she hung up the phone and went off in search of her husband.

She found him in the giant bathroom, lighting candles. He was in his shirtsleeves, his tie off and his feet bare. The bathroom smelled of him and only him and she relaxed.

"Hi."

He turned. "Hello there. Everything fine with Cascadia?"

"Oh yeah. Great. They're all very happy and will be there tomorrow night. But enough about them. I'm so glad you're still clothed because I want to see you strip for me."

She stood there in the doorway, watching him, delighting in the way his breath hitched.

"Only if I get the same treat," he said, walking toward her, hand slowly popping the buttons on his shirt open.

"Oh don't worry, by the time you pass out, you'll know where all my tattoos are."

He stopped for a moment and laughed. "I do like your sense of humor, Tracy."

"If it gets you naked faster, I've got loads more material up here." She tapped her temple and he grinned just before he let his shirt fall from his body and stood there, candlelight gleaming off his skin. Like most wolves whose ancestors came to the Americas in the Diaspora, his roots were southern European. His hair was dark and his skin had an olive tone.

His upper body was perfectly proportioned. Wide shoulders with layers of hard, compact muscle tapered into a V shape with a narrow waist and flat abdomen. He had just the right amount of hair on his chest, not too much but not hairless either.

"My. What a lucky wolf I am. The pants too," she murmured as she took the sight of him in.

He unbuckled his belt, undid his pants and let them slide to the floor and shoved the boxer briefs down. To say that he was well endowed would be an understatement. She'd only seen the briefest of glimpses of his cock earlier and had certainly felt it fill her up, but the whole package made her a bit lightheaded.

"Do you like what you see?"

She nodded mutely. There were no words and even if there were, she wasn't sure she'd be able to form them in the dryness of her mouth. He was beautiful. Beautiful and masculine and big and strong and oh-so tough. She shivered at the sight of him. She saw him notice her reaction and his smile in return was filled with sexy promise.

"Now you. Show me your tattoos."

Grabbing the hem of her shirt, she yanked it up and over her head, tossing it to the side. She'd toed off her boots in the other room and now she unceremoniously shucked her jeans, panties and socks.

"Damn but you're gorgeous. Those freckles like sprinkled cinnamon across your nose and cheeks belie the naughty girl the piercings expose. I like that." He approached her and cupped her breasts. "And these little breasts are delicious."

If anyone else had said "little breasts" to her, she'd have died on the spot, but coming from him, it was a compliment.

He traced a finger to her shoulder where one of her tattoos was. "This is pretty."

"It's in the old language. It means 'liberation'."

He laved his tongue over it and she shivered.

"And this one?" he asked, touching the one at the inside of her hip.

"That one is Sheela Na Gig. A goddess of life."

"Hmm, very fitting." He traced the outline of the little round goddess. "Where else?"

She held out her wrists and showed him the insides. Those tattoos, too, were in the old language. "This one is destiny. And this one is courage." He pressed a kiss to each one and those eyes pulled back to her own again.

She turned slowly and looked back at him over her shoulder. "That one is a raven."

He bent to look at it more closely. It was more than that, it was a raven on the back of a wolf. "This is beautiful, Tracy."

"Thank you. When I was ten I had this series of dreams and I kept changing into a raven and as the raven has such a big part to play in our own mythological structure, it's always stuck with me as sort of my touchstone animal."

In werewolf mythology, the raven was the source of knowledge, a guide in all things.

He couldn't quite believe how utterly turned on he was by her body. He'd never in a million years been attracted to women with piercings and tattoos and yet this one turned him on past bearing. He loved that edge about her, loved her naughtiness, and it made him feel that way too. Certainly he was no prude but he'd never had sex outside in a hedge maze. He'd never seen a tattoo on someone and wanted to lick it.

Unable to resist, he licked each tiny dimple at the base of her spine and she gasped. Standing, he moved around her, so hard his cock tapped his stomach. "Champagne and chocolate and a bath await you."

Stepping in, he held out a hand and she took it, letting him help her into the tub. Sitting in the water across from him, she sighed, her eyes going half-lidded. "This bathtub is something else. My house was built in the Forties, the bathtub is very utilitarian. This is a sex bathtub."

"It is with you in it. I can't say I've used it for sex or taking a bath even. But seeing you here with the water running down your body, all wet and glistening, makes me reevaluate my position on that."

He handed her a glass of champagne and touched his own to it. "To us."

"To us," she echoed back and took a drink. "Very nice."

"Thank you. I've had this bottle since I graduated from business school. I'm glad I had something worthy of you."

"Flatterer. You're so getting lucky."

He looked surprised for a moment and then laughed. "I already have."

He picked up a chocolate from the gold box and moved toward her with it. Thinking he'd feed it to her, she leaned in.

"Oh no, I'm eating this one," he said as he brushed the truffle over a hard nipple, smearing it across her flesh. Because they already had a high body core temperature and the water was so warm, it melted against her skin, a ribbon of chocolate trickling down her nipple.

"Mmmmm," she murmured inarticulately. She'd been about to say it was a waste of good Godiva chocolate but she changed her mind when his tongue swirled around her areola to taste it and her too.

"You've got some moves on you, I must say."

"You're troublesome, aren't you?" He scraped the edge of his teeth over her nipple and she sighed, arching into him.

"Am I supposed to…oh yes right there…pretend that you haven't been a rake, a rogue, a bounder?"

She felt his lips curve up into a smile, his mouth still on her nipple. "In any case…oh god yes…I think I quite appreciate all those years of preparation to please me."

"Are you always this full of shit?" he asked, kissing across her chest to her other breast.

"I am," she assured him. "It's a comfort to you, I'm sure, to give up the fast lane and the fast women with their designer clothes, big breasts and long legs." She reached down with a hand slick with the oil he'd put in the water and slid her palm up and down his cock idly as she spoke.

"My darling, there are no other women." And he meant it.

She laughed, throaty and sexy, and he pulled her into his lap, astride him. "There'd better not be. Because the freckles may fool you, but I'd kill you if you strayed." Her lips curved up on the left and created a devastating dimple.

"Oh, you dirty talker, you." He gasped as she reached back and positioned him. Instead of thrusting up into her he picked her up, sitting her on the side of the tub, standing and stepping out.

"No, not yet. I want to see you stretched out on our bed, looking down at me as I taste you."

Smiling to himself at the way her eyes had widened and then gone half-lidded at his statement, he dried himself quickly and turned back to help her dry off. "I've put us in the guest room for the night while our bedroom airs out. Is that all right?"

She grabbed the champagne and the glasses and nodded. "More than all right. Thank you, Nick."

He pushed open the door to a smaller but still very nicely decorated bedroom. She moved past him, putting the stuff down on the bedside table, tossing her towel over a chair. His soon joined it.

"I'm sorry about that, you know," he said, pushing her back on the mattress.

She put a finger over his lips. "Don't. It's all right. You didn't know. I think there are better things to think about than that, don't you?"

He nodded and sucked her finger into his mouth, tongue swirling around it until she gasped. He slowly pulled back and leaned in, lips close to hers. "Earlier I showed absolutely no finesse and I'm appalled at that. To think that our first time together was so fast. I think I need to show you what you can look forward to every day for the rest of your life."

She rose up and licked over his lips. "Go on with your bad self. But it wasn't *fast*. It was hot. And fevered. And *oh my god I can't help myself I have to fuck you so back against the wall now*. And that, my darling, isn't fast, that's divine."

"Put that way, I may be able to live with it. But let's see what I can do about easing your condition." His hand slid down and agile fingers found her pussy. "Oh, darling, you seem to be very wet."

She knew there was a saucy remark in her somewhere, but damned if she could move her lips to say it. Instead her head fell back to the pillows and she widened her thighs in invitation.

Rising over her, he placed a trail of kisses over her collarbone. He took his time, leisurely moving, breathing her in, committing each inch of her skin to memory. Her pulse beat frantically beneath his lips when he kissed the hollow of her throat.

He continued on, kissing down her chest and over each perky pink nipple. He vowed to get her some pretty rings with diamonds hanging from them, maybe even pink diamonds to match those damned delicious little nipples.

A gasp broke from her as she arched into him when he took the ring between his teeth, sending shivers down his spine. Her nipples hardened and stabbed into his mouth and palm. He kissed and nibbled and licked until all she could do was writhe and make whispered entreaties.

Leaving her nipples behind, he kissed down the curve and over each rib, stopping to flick his tongue around her navel, and he settled himself between her thighs.

Spreading her smooth, bare pussy open, he looked his fill. So pretty, glistening pink. Her clit was hard and swollen and he moved closer to give it a lick. Her taste shocked him. He had to close his eyes for a moment as it careened through his body. She was perfect, tangy and salty and fresh—his. It was like she was written into his system, like a basic operating language, and everything in his life just clicked into place.

He watched as he traced the furls of her pussy with a fingertip and slid inside. Another finger and a third squeezed in and she was rolling her hips and gasping his name.

His mouth covered her, devoured her and his ears were greedy for her gasps, for the sound of her nails clutching at the sheets. Her juicy flesh swelled for him and he hooked his fingers and stroked that sweet spot over and over again until she reared up, back bowed, thighs clamped over his ears and screamed her climax.

On and on she rode it, body electric with pleasure until at last it left her boneless and she fell back against the bed and her thighs dropped, freeing him.

Her face was satisfied and serene when he looked up at her.

"That was quite nice," she said, a smirk on her lips.

"Yeah? Well, I've got a few more tricks in my bag. You still with me?"

"Oh yes, dazzle me."

He moved up her body until he was nose to nose with her. "There you are," he murmured and she reached up to kiss him.

"Never far away. You planning on doing anything with that wonderfully thick cock? Like say, putting it into me?"

"Like this?" he asked as he thrust into her to the root in one hard movement.

Her back bowed and her legs wrapped around his waist. "That'll do quite nicely."

They were nearly the same height so they stayed nose to nose while he began to move into her. Their eyes remained locked and it felt like she saw into his very soul. He felt exposed and wondered if she'd like what she saw there.

Her body embraced him, pulled him back each time he pulled out, she was so tight and hot that he felt like he'd lose his mind. He wanted to crawl into her and curl up. She was long and lean with a nice ass and it felt like she was made for him, to be beneath him, to receive his body this very way.

When she tightened her vaginal muscles around his cock he grunted and his balls pulled tight against his body. She rolled her hips up to meet his thrusts.

"Baby, touch yourself. Make yourself come around my cock."

He watched her hands as she pressed her breasts together and pulled on the rings on her nipples. He moaned as he felt the ripple of her pussy around him and saw the way she'd caught her bottom lip between her teeth.

Down one hand went, moving between them, and he felt her pull her honey up and around her clit.

"Tell me how it feels."

"Good," she gasped. "My clit is so hard and your cock is so hard and you're filling me up. You make me so wet. Fuck me, Nick. Come inside me and mark me. Make me yours."

Holy crap, the woman was so sexy it made his head hurt. His wolf was rolling through him, pressing against hers. His climax was building and suddenly it hurtled through him, the impact shocking and mind-numbing.

His head went back and a howl of her name ripped from his lips. Dimly, he felt her come beneath him, their bodies moving in and toward and away and against the other over and over until he collapsed.

"Ungh," she mumbled and he nodded, his head on her shoulder.

* * * * *

She awoke some hours later to find herself alone in bed and sat up slowly, stretching. Grabbing a robe that she found hanging on the back of the door, she went out in search of him.

He was in his office, on the phone. She heard his end perfectly. Her hearing was good enough to catch part of the other end of the call and she stood there, wanting to scream.

"I don't know. I still care about you, but now that she's here it's not as strong. I love her. She's my mate."

"…love you still…not me…"

"No, she's not you. She's different. I'm sorry I called you. I just wanted to share this with you. But I see that it's hard for you and not fair to her."

Tracy stood in the doorway, waiting.

"I need to get back to bed."

"…skinny…eyebrow!…"

"This isn't…" he ran a frustrated hand through his hair, "I need to go. I'll see you tomorrow night. Or I guess tonight."

The woman on the other end said something else and Nick sighed and hung up. He put his head down but looked up when he heard her move.

"Tracy," he began, seeing her there.

"Sarah." She said it simply.

"I…"

"Fuck you, Nick. God damn it. Fuck you and fuck her!"

"It's not what you think." He stood up and walked toward her and she scrambled backward, hand out to ward him off. He stopped, hurt. "Don't run from me. Do you think I'd hurt you?"

"You already did, you bastard. You and that blonde bitch. God, how stupid am I? I come in here and your bed reeks of another woman's pussy! I should have known. I saw the way she looked at you."

"Shelley has nothing to do with this."

Incredulous, Tracy picked up a book on the table near where she was standing and hurled it at his head. "No, you stupid asshole! That bitch Sarah, not your fuck buddy."

"Hey!" He batted the book away. "Nothing happened between me and Sarah. I just wanted to share this with her."

"You called someone else's wife at," she craned her neck to see the clock, "four in the morning, Nick! I heard her, I'm skinny? My brow ring offends her? Fuck her! Her talking to my mate when he should be in bed with me offends me!"

"She wasn't serious. It's hard for her."

"Oh you are *not* making excuses for her to me, are you? I thought you said you had a lot of experience with women. Here's a clue, *don't defend her to me if you want to keep your head.*"

"I'm not defending her. I'm her anchor. For the last few years I've been sort of her husband too. Platonic. Nothing has happened between us since the tri-bond. But it's intense. A part of me loved her, felt mated to her." He took a step closer. "Until you. Tracy, the moment I touched you that bond, or that part of it, weakened. She's my sister-in-law and I'm her anchor and in that way, we'll still be close. But I love you."

She shook her head. "You said it yourself, Nick. I'm not her. And I wouldn't want to be. And I don't want to be with you knowing that when you close your eyes you're thinking of her."

"You aren't her. That's not an insult! You're different. You're full of life and you have an edge and you're more independent and you're stronger in a lot of ways. And I love you. I swear to you that when I close my eyes I see you. When my eyes are open I see you. Why can't you believe me?"

"Because you left a bed with me in it to call her."

He took a step toward her and she moved back and he growled at her. "Don't. Tracy, my wolf is so close to the surface right now. Please, don't hold yourself back from me."

"I don't want you to touch me."

He closed his eyes. "This isn't the way it's supposed to go."

"Oh, should I stand there and look vacant like Sarah? Would that be amenable to you?"

"Can we stop this and work things out please? We're in the same Pack, she's your Alpha."

"Not if I don't join your Pack. Right now my Alpha is Cade Warden and Cascadia is looking better and better by the second."

He froze. "What? You're not being rational. I'm sorry I hurt you. I woke up and wanted to share this with someone. I was happy, damn you! I wanted to call someone who is my best friend to share it with her. She's up early because she does financial analysis and gets up with the markets in New York."

"And yet, your *best friend* talked smack about me and you what? Lost your tongue? If anyone spoke ill of you I'd have cut them off at the knees."

"She's jealous, damn it! She doesn't mean it. She likes you and she wants me to be happy. And you make me happy. Or you do sometimes when you're not insane. Tracy, you're my mate."

"Well, I don't like her. And I don't like you leaving me to call her. And I don't like you not defending me. And I don't like your fucking apartment with its white carpets and furniture that looks like I can't sit on it and I want my dog and my family and my business! I have nothing here. No friends, no family, nothing, and you don't seem to get that."

"This apartment is perfect for me, Tracy. My gym is just a few blocks' walk and the Pack offices are half a mile away. All my favorite restaurants are close by."

She looked at him and shook her head. "You're unbelievable. You. You. You. This apartment is perfect for *you.* *Your* gym is close. *Your* job is close and let's not forget *your* favorite restaurants. Forgive me! Oh and let's not forget about *your* best friend. Well, Nick, you can keep *your* apartment and your best friend and your stupid messed-up Pack. I'm going back to Seattle."

She turned on her heel and stormed out of the room, Nick on her heels.

He caught up with her, the weight of his body bringing her down to the bed. He remained on top of her, holding her in place. "You're right! Okay? I've been a selfish asshole. You *are* giving up everything. We'll buy a house and your dog can come live with us. Don't leave me, Tracy. Not when I've found you. I love you. I want to be with you. Not Sarah. I swear to you. It was *never* about that. I called to share this thing with her because she has it too and I just wanted to marvel over it."

She felt his heart pounding against her chest, heard the sincerity in his voice. But it hurt. Hearing that call hurt and she didn't know what to do about it.

"Please. Baby, let's work this out. Forgive me."

He put his forehead on hers and the tears came from her gut with a gasp.

"Oh, love, god, I've made you cry. I'm sorry. I'm so sorry. How can I make it better? Tell me."

"I don't know. How can I trust you? I can't. And *her*, I don't want to be in a Pack with her. I don't want to be in the same state with her."

"You can trust me, Tracy. I haven't violated your trust from the first moment I touched you. Surely you can feel me through the bond. You must know I'm telling you the truth."

She didn't know what to think. She did feel a bit on edge and a bit crazy over it. She wanted to hurt Sarah for saying that stuff about her and for trying to undermine her with Nick.

"Perhaps. But you went to her and you stayed silent when she spoke poorly of me. How can I let that be my Alpha? In comparison, well, there is no comparison. Cade is a hundred times better than that. Nina, who is the highest-level female, who outranks me, is not sneaky and cruel. Why would

I trade that for your Pack? Why would I trade Cascadia for Pacific?"

"I'm sorry I didn't say anything. But you don't know her. She was just blowing off steam. She didn't mean any of it. If I thought she did, I would have said something. If she ever would have said anything negative about you again, I'd definitely defend you. But this whole thing has been an adjustment for everyone. You aren't anchored to anyone. I can't explain it to you but certainly, Cade and Nina must be close."

"Yes. And I've seen the way he looks at her and that's what worries me."

"Cade isn't mated yet. When he finds his mate the intensity of his love and desire for Nina will fade. That's what happened to me. Plus, Cade, Lex and Nina live together. I've made it a point to live across the city. I'm trying to be honest with you about all of this."

His eyes were earnest and his voice was sincere. She could hear the pain in it at having hurt her as well as being hurt himself.

"Please don't leave, Tracy. Stay here with me. Love me and let me love you."

She took a deep breath. "I do love you. That's why it hurt so much to hear that phone call."

"If I could redo some of my actions from the last two days, I would. We'd be in my...our bed right now and I wouldn't have made that call. But I can't turn back time. All I can do is ask you to hold on with me through all of this so we can continue to move forward and grow together. Because I want you so much. I need you. I love you."

Reaching up, she sifted fingertips through his hair. "One step at a time. I'm no longer contemplating calling my grandma to ask her if those stories about magic to break a mate bond are true. I want you too. I love you. But I'm not sure about anything past that."

"What do you mean?" Despite the serious nature of the discussion he was hard and found himself wanting her yet again. Wanting the lovemaking to heal the rift.

"I mean that if I join Pacific I have to pledge an oath to the Pack and to the Alphas and I can't pledge anything but that I want to pull that fake blonde hair off that bitch's head."

"Wow." He fought a grin. She was so pissed off and jealous. It affected him in a very primal way. She was a vicious little wolf and his wolf liked that.

She rolled her eyes but couldn't help a little roll of her hips. "Don't tell me this whole girlfight thing is making you hot."

"No, it's not about her. It's about you being so willing to kick the ass of anyone you think is threatening your bond with me. Which you're totally wrong about, by the way. I happen to like long, lean, lithe women with tattoos and wicked tempers."

"Do you think flattery is going to get you out of this?"

He laughed. "You're a hard case, Tracy. So you won't kill me in my sleep and you're willing to stay and be my mate?" He suspected that part of why her feelings were so intense was the lack of the tri-bond. He hoped that after it was in place she'd feel more centered and sure. The idea of him wanting Sarah over her was ludicrous. He was sure he wouldn't have thought so a week ago, but Tracy cast a deep shadow, there was no comparison.

"And we are going to start looking for a house tomorrow." Tracy's look dared him to argue.

He was no fool. Nodding, he agreed. "Okay. And the joining?"

"I don't know, Nick. I can't swear fealty to her. I can punch her, though."

His mind raced at how he'd deal with this situation. She'd mortally offend the Pack if she refused the joining. But knowing her, she'd say exactly why and the Pack would be angry with Sarah and Nick as well. And Ben would be left holding the bag and trying to figure out how to fix it all. Plus, damn it, he wanted her in his Pack not Cascadia. He wanted to share his rank with her, wanted her in his family.

"One step at a time, baby. For now, I have a suggestion." He raised his eyebrows at her and she laughed but didn't stop him when his hands pushed the front of her robe open.

Chapter Three

ຂໆ

Gabe had been awake since five, when his dreams of Tracy Warden ended and his thoughts of her began.

He loved the whole concept of the anchor. Over the years he'd had the opportunity here and there but had said no. He most definitely wanted to be someone's anchor but he'd always felt like the woman would have to be someone very, very special to him.

Gabe readily admitted to himself that his offer to be Tracy's anchor was self-serving. He wanted her. Had wanted her since the first time he'd clapped eyes on her in that room the morning before. Instantly, the sight and smell of her had shot to his gut.

Because she was mated to Nick, he'd certainly not have the opportunity to see her naked in any other way. And admittedly, that was frustrating. If there was no mate bond, Gabe would have no problem whatsoever doing whatever he could to grab Tracy for himself.

But he hadn't expected to want to be anchored to a woman like Tracy. His attraction to her, the depth and intensity of it surprised him. Shocked him even. She fascinated him. Wound her way into his brain in a way no other female ever had. At first he'd surprised himself by offering to be their anchor. He'd said it without really thinking about it. The words just burst from him. He wasn't sure why he felt as deeply as he did and now he really wasn't sure if it was wise to be bonded to her in even an ancillary way. He was a man who valued control and his attraction to Tracy made him feel out of control.

He'd mulled it in his head, paced, and once in his bed, tossed and turned a long time. In the end, his decision was to roll with it. Because Gabe wanted to know Tracy more.

Sure, it was attractive that she came from a very powerful and revered family. As a human who'd been transformed and had been looking from the outside in for most of his adult life he had to admit that such things mattered in the world of wolves. Being anchored to a woman as powerful as Tracy Warden brought his status up as a former human. Even though he was one of the most highly ranked werewolves in the country, her coming from such a powerful family mattered in werewolf culture.

But that wasn't it. Not even a small part. No, he liked the idea of being as special to her as she'd be to him. Having that connection to her made him warm inside. He'd been happy these last twenty years as a wolf, but he had missed that connection since his mentor had died.

He liked the Northwest and now he'd have a reason to visit more frequently. As her anchor, he'd be a part of her life forever, even after he himself bonded with his mate. As an anchor he'd be like a member of her family. He smiled as his body tightened in anticipation.

* * * * *

Over coffee several hours after Tracy and Nick had made up, they sat curled into each other on the couch, watching the morning out of the windows.

"So, uh, I hate to bring this up and all, but isn't Gabe going to be here soon?"

"Yeah, in about an hour." He hated the idea of her with anyone else and knowing that the scent of her sex with another male would be in the air, he really hated the idea that it would happen there. Perhaps it was a good thing he'd agreed to move.

Tracy told him about the whole tri-bond fiasco between Nina, Lex and Cade.

"Well, as a human, I'm sure it was harder for Nina at the time. I *understand* why it has to happen and on that level I'm okay with it. I want to protect you. I need to. But there is this sliver of unease inside me at the thought of my mate with someone else."

"How can we make this easier for you?" She wished she could forego it entirely, seeing how he felt about it. But she also felt herself slipping a bit as the time passed. Felt the encroaching dark place. "Do you want to be in the room? In the apartment? Do you want to go for a workout and then come back afterwards?"

"Part of me wants to be far, far away but another part of me knows I'd imagine all sorts of things if I wasn't here. I do think I need to not be in the room though. It's going to be an issue that he's not related to me *and* that he outranks me. I'll work in my office. When it's over, we have to talk about the joining."

Tracy stiffened. "What is that all about? You're pissed because of the tri-bond and you bring that up to get back at me?"

He turned and looked her in the eyes. "No. Tracy, I am not passive-aggressive. If I have an issue you'll know it. But we do have to talk about it and I'd like to see if perhaps you'll be more…adjusted after you have an anchor."

She narrowed her eyes at him. "Are you suggesting that I'm overreacting to my mate sneaking out of bed at four a.m. to call another woman who he professed to have deep feelings for?"

"I'm not saying you're wrong for being upset. It was a mistake, I admit that and I've apologized for it. But I do think your reaction was rather severe and I'm hoping that after the tri-bond you're more centered and we can pick it up again. In any case, we'll have to because the joining is tonight."

"Scheduled for tonight, that is. And I'd like to know how you'd react if our positions were reversed."

He got quiet as he thought about it.

She got up and kissed him on the top of his head. "I'm going to take a shower and, uh, prepare for Gabe."

He stood and trailed after her into the bathroom.

She laughed as she slipped out of her robe. His hands found their way to her body again. "Don't start anything right now. You're the reason I have to shower again as it is."

He hopped up on the counter and watched as she got into the glass enclosure. "Tracy, I've been thinking, and I want you to let go and enjoy yourself with Gabe. I mean, it's the last time you'll ever have sex with someone other than me and I want you to get off."

She wiped her hand through the steam and looked out at him.

"I'm serious. I want you to have this. I don't want it to be clinical and uncomfortable." What he didn't say was that Ben had said the same thing to Sarah and had gone to another part of the house, leaving her with Nick. And it had been even more special because of that. He wanted Tracy and Gabe to have that connection. And it was easy enough to say because Gabe didn't live in the same city, much less the same state. Yes, Gabe would be a part of their lives forever, but it was easier with some distance.

"Well, we'll see." She sounded dubious.

After she got out of the shower she stayed in a robe and changed the sheets in the guest bedroom and tried not to show how nervous she was as Nick watched her.

She brewed some coffee and he helped her make a nice breakfast and set the table as she bustled around.

They both jumped when a knock sounded on the door and Nick squeezed her hand before going to answer it.

Gabe was there in jeans and a black cashmere sweater, looking suave and effortlessly, classically handsome and Nick only barely stopped himself from narrowing an eye at him.

Instead he stood back and motioned Gabe inside with a sweep of his hand. "Gabe, good morning. Please come in. Tracy is just finishing up the crêpes."

Gabe's eyes widened a bit as he came into the apartment. "Crêpes? I do believe you're even luckier than I'd thought."

Tracy laughed as she heard that comment, putting the crêpes on the table with a tea towel covering them to keep them warm.

"Hi, Gabe. Please sit down."

He went to her and kissed her cheek and it sent a shiver down her spine. He smelled good and he was warm against her body.

"Thank you, Tracy. This all looks marvelous." He pulled out a chair, careful to avoid the one at the head of the table, and sat down.

"Please, help yourself to coffee. The different fillings are all here in reach." She blinked quickly, nervous beyond belief.

He reached out and grabbed her hand. "Tracy, this is going to be all right. We'll just take it slow and step-by-step. The three of us will work this through."

"Thank you." A blush crept up her neck and Nick smiled at her, relaxing her a bit.

Gabe filled his plate and tried not to look at her too much. She was alluring there in her robe. Her hair curled softly about her face and shoulders and unless he was wrong, there was not a stitch beneath the silk of the robe.

After a leisurely breakfast, where the three of them got on quite nicely, he put his napkin on the table and looked at Nick.

"How shall we proceed?"

"I'm going to finish up some work in my office. If I need to, I'll duck out. I've discussed with Tracy that I want this to be a pleasurable experience for her so take it for what that's worth."

"Hello? Does anyone want to, oh, I don't know, address me? Or shall I stand over here and look pretty while you divvy up my pussy?"

Both men looked to her, shocked momentarily. Gabe fought back a laugh at her impertinence and bold words.

"I do apologize, Tracy. Is there anything you'd like to add or say?"

"Well, I do want to make it known that I am not on board with the way wolves think females are just there to sit in the background and look vacant and breed on. I have a degree in economics, you know. And if we're all going to be bonded, it's good to get this all straight from the beginning."

Gabe nodded. "I agree, actually. I wasn't born a wolf. There are many human conventions that I still hold. And lucky for me, I happen to like strong females. I did not mean for my addressing Nick to seem that I was ignoring your input on this issue."

"Tracy has such trouble expressing herself." Nick's voice was dry but his eyes were full of amused adoration and Gabe and Tracy both relaxed at the sight.

"Hmpf!" Tracy smirked at them both.

"And on that very articulate note, I will take this coffee into my office to work. And my headphones." Nick stood and went to Tracy, who stood up and went into his arms. "I love you," he murmured into her hair, breathing her scent in and letting it calm him.

"I love you too. Are you sure you're okay with this?" She tipped her head back and looked into his eyes.

He nodded. "The tri-bond is an old thing with us. Without it, you'd be lost to me and to yourself. I'm all right." He turned to Gabe and they shook hands. "Take care of her. I am indebted to you for being our anchor."

Gabe nodded. "It is my honor to do so."

Nick grabbed the carafe of coffee, headed down the opposite hallway to his office and firmly shut his door.

Tracy turned to Gabe, suddenly shy. She held out her hand. "Shall we?"

He took it and the connection arced up their arms, bringing a gasp from both their lips.

She led him into the room and closed the door behind her, looking at him. God he was beautiful. He was taller than Nick but not hard-bodied. A long torso and legs. The jeans he wore highlighted the power in the thighs that most werewolves had and it had always been one of the most appealing features on a man's body to Tracy.

Salt-and-pepper sprinkled just a bit at the temples of his caramel-colored hair. It was short, professional, but not too short. Enough to run her fingers through. His eyes were deep brown, nearly black and he had the smallest hint of wrinkles around the outer corners. They were serious eyes but she'd noticed a twinkle of amusement in them from time to time. A streak of whimsy was a wonderful quality in a man with such a serious position.

He had a neatly trimmed mustache and beard that seemed to frame his lips. His lips were the only utterly soft thing about his face. She licked her own lips in response as her body reacted to the fleshy curve of his bottom lip.

She watched as he reached down and pulled his sweater up and over his head. His chest was impressive. Again, not hard muscle like Nick's, Nick was a man whose body was a weapon, a tool in his job. Nick's body was a killing machine. Gabe's chest belonged to a man who kept himself well. It was nicely defined and more of that sexy salt-and-pepper spread over the chest hair and the arrow of hair around his navel and disappeared beneath his waistband.

"I'm incredibly flattered," he murmured.

She couldn't help but grin. "You should be. Because I'm beginning to entertain some really naughty thoughts about you."

"How old are you?"

"Twenty-five. And you?"

"Forty-one. I'm a lot older than you are. I feel slightly perverted."

She dropped the robe, letting it pool around her feet, the spill of royal blue silk like an expanse of sea.

"Okay, now I'm feeling a lot perverted." He wondered if he'd ever actually been as hard as he was at that precise moment. How long had it been since a woman's body had affected him so deeply? She was a whole lot of contradictions all rolled up into one really appealing package. The freckles gave her an almost pixieish look combined with that nose with the tiny upturn at the end. Her eyes were wide and bright and definitely filled with mischief. The green reminded him of moss.

Her breasts were not large. He usually preferred large-breasted women, but her perky little barely B-cups made his mouth water. Those strawberry-pink nipples with silver—platinum, he guessed, given their resistance to silver—rings dangling from them made him hot. No innocent miss there. No, those rings made him want to unleash the things he'd kept deep inside him for a very long time. He raked his eyes over the series of tattoos—words from the old language—down her body, over those long legs to the petite feet with those red-hot painted nails. She was a lot of things in one woman and that was incredibly beguiling.

"You're so beautiful," he said in the quietest of voices and she stood, rapt, as his hands went to the buttons of his jeans and popped each one open. She wasn't even sure she could blush, she was so spellbound by the sound as each button popped free and a tiny bit more of his body showed.

My! No underwear. Who'd have thought that a man like Gabe, who seemed all business, would be going commando? A shiver ran through her. He shoved the pants off and got rid of them and his shoes and socks.

They stood there facing each other, both naked and intensely aroused. Somewhere in the back of her mind she felt guilty for being this turned on by another male and it seemed odd to her that with the mate bond she could be so utterly devastated by his presence. She chalked it up to the whole anchor thing. She couldn't explain it any other way.

"I really have to touch you, Tracy."

She nodded and stepped out of the robe at her feet, toward him. And when their bodies touched, Tracy felt faint. The intensity of desire and connection between them was overwhelming.

"What is this?" he murmured just as his hand went into her hair and angled her head to receive his kiss. And it wasn't just a kiss, it was a ten-car pileup. A collision of two people meshing into one. His mouth was insistent and he devoured her, took from her and delivered back in spades. His lips were hot against hers, tongue sure and steady as it slid into her mouth and stroked against hers.

His taste was intoxicating and consumed her. Took over her brain and her body and sucked her under like a siren's song.

"Oh, god. Please, fuck me, Gabe," she all but sobbed when he broke the kiss to move his mouth—his hot, carnal mouth—to the spot just under her ear. Her legs nearly buckled.

"I will, little rebel, I will. Don't rush me." The words were murmured, his lips against her skin, and all she could do was writhe. "I have plans for every inch of your body. If I can only have you once, I'm going to burn my name into your skin."

He wasn't even sure where the hell the words came from but once he'd touched her, it was like instinct had taken over.

He certainly meant what he'd said. He wanted her to think of his lips just there, at the place where her jaw met her neck, before she fell asleep each night. Wanted his fingers splayed over her hips to brand into her memory forever because damn it, if he couldn't have her, he'd damn well have part of her memory.

A sense of desperation crept into him as the thought of only having her once registered. How could he live for the rest of his life only being able to make love to her one time? Knowing that another man had her every night and day? He knew it was madness to feel that way, knew she belonged to another. But he felt it nonetheless.

Dropping to his knees before her, he caught the scent of her desire in full force and it rocked his very foundations. He growled as his wolf agitated against his human skin, wanting to claim her.

Tracy looked down at him, her hands shaking at the intensity of her response. She slid them into his hair and it felt cool and soft against her skin. His mouth was like a brand against the tattoo at her inner hip. The growl that issued from deep inside him wrapped around her and called her own wolf into a state of tension and need. It frightened her, the way he made her feel. It was wrong! She shouldn't feel so intensely attracted to anyone but Nick. But she couldn't help it. Her need of him took over every cell in her body. Did Nina feel this way with Cade? No wonder she looked at him the way she did sometimes. Still, Nina seemed to manage it and be loving and totally devoted to Lex. All Tracy could do was hope that it would lessen after the anchor bond was fully in place.

He pushed her back onto the bed and moved to her, giving no quarter as he loomed up and over her, taking a nipple into his mouth, his teeth grabbing it, pushing her into that place where pleasure and pain are only a breath apart.

Her clit throbbed in time with each pull of his mouth. His weight over her eased some of the anxiety she'd been feeling.

His hands were stroking over every inch of her skin as he feasted on her nipples.

Pulling back, his lips were wet from her and his breath was heaving. "What is it? Why do you make me feel this way?"

She was beyond words and all she could do was shake her head and make a distressed sound. He kissed his way down her belly and her thighs were already trembling when he pushed them all the way open and took a long look at her pussy.

"God," he whispered hoarsely and his mouth was there on her, against her, insistent and fervent. She'd already been so close to coming just at his first touch that when he pushed a finger into her and flicked the tip of his tongue over her clit her climax hit her so hard it jarred her teeth.

But he didn't stop until he'd pushed her into a second climax that wrenched her gut and made her see stars.

And he was up and over her again, lips on hers. Her legs wrapped around his waist and she opened to him, tightening her grip to hold him to her.

"Please," she said through the kiss.

"Please what?"

"Please fuck me. I'm going to die if you don't."

"I don't want this to be over." The yearning in his voice tore at her.

"It has to be. I can't feel like this, it's not right." Tracy knew that this thing between her and Gabe was something other than the anchor bond. Knew that it was deeper than that and it scared her as much as it seduced her. She had a mate, he was in the other room and she was in love with him and committed to him and she could not let herself fall any further into this thing she shared with Gabe.

"I know. But damn me, I want it forever," he gasped as he pushed his cock deep into her hot embrace.

"Oh, my…" she said faintly as he filled her and began to move. She closed her eyes to keep from staring deep into his. It was too much. He saw into her too deeply and she didn't know what to do with all of it.

Each time he plunged back into her body she felt like he possessed a bit more of her. She pushed the panic down, worried that if she didn't, Nick would feel it and burst into the room and then what?

The pleasure was mind-numbing and all-consuming and she tried to turn off her mind and heart and just feel.

Gabe was convinced he'd never felt anything as good as the way her pussy surrounded his cock as he fucked into her body. The silk of the skin on her inner thighs slid over his hips each time he thrust deep. He wanted her to open her eyes, to see into those mossy depths and know her. Her body welcomed him in a way he'd never felt before and even clenching his teeth and reciting his mnemonics from the bar exam for commercial paper did not help.

He had to come and right then. His cock didn't care if he wasn't ready for it to be over. Her body had pushed him past endurance and when it hit him square in the balls, it also hit him in his heart, in his gut and he threw his head back and gasped out her name as he came deep within her body in pulse after pulse of pleasure.

He stayed inside her as long as he could and finally rolled to the side, chest heaving, his arm over her waist, fingers entwined with hers.

After some minutes of silence, he moved to sit and leaned down to kiss her. His eyes were sad. It tore at her and she wanted to make him all right. Wanted to comfort him. But she couldn't. It wasn't her place.

"I'm going. I'll see you tonight at the joining." He paused a moment, tracing a fingertip over her bottom lip. "It's just the anchor forming, Tracy. That's all."

She looked into those deep brown eyes and nodded. "Of course. Thank you."

He laughed as he got up and pulled his clothes on. "Sweetness, thank you. I quite enjoyed myself. I'll be happy to get to know you better as your anchor." He went to the door and turned to her one last time. "It was just the bond."

He said it twice but she wasn't any more reassured. She just hoped that the bond lessened because she wanted him again, his hands on her. Right then. Pushing it away as hard as she could, she nodded. "Of course. I'll see you later tonight, Gabe."

He waved and left the room, shutting the door behind him.

Gabe walked straight out of the apartment, knowing that he smelled of Tracy's sex and her body and that if he'd gone to Nick right then it would have been hard on him. From what he understood, most of the time the anchor left for a while to let the mated couple reassert their bond anyway.

Or so he told himself as he tried to put as much distance between himself and Tracy as possible before he let his wolf take over and challenge Nick Lawrence for his mate.

* * * * *

Her thoughts racing and unease gripping her guts, Tracy threw herself into changing the sheets on the bed and opening the windows. She wanted to try and get rid of the scent for Nick's sake. And for her own.

Giving herself a bunch of tasks was better than thinking about what had happened. She showered and tried to erase Gabe's scent from her skin, but she couldn't erase the memory of his touch, the way his lips had felt on her own. He had burned himself into her, just like he said he wanted to. Guilt beat at her.

She loved Nick. Period. She loved Nick Lawrence and she was his mate. She was just unaccustomed to the whole anchor bond thing. Still, she'd talk to Nina about it when she saw her at the Pacific Pack house later that night.

An hour later, scrubbed and calmer, the bedroom airing out, Tracy sought Nick out.

Standing in the doorway, she watched him work. Took in the expanse of his back, of the way the muscles moved as he typed. His hands were really beautiful for a man who'd probably broken a finger or two at least half a dozen times. He was wearing headphones and listening to his mp3 player but she could tell he was distracted. She tossed a paperclip at his head and he jumped and turned in her direction.

When he saw it was her though, he relaxed and took the ear buds out and smiled. "Hey. Is everything okay?"

"Yeah. How about you?"

He stood and walked to her, relieved that there was only a slight scent of sex on her. He'd heard when Gabe left the apartment and had given her time. The washing machine was on in the distance and he smelled fresh air and he had to give a rueful smile that she had to air out a bedroom in much the same way he had.

"You feel more centered than you did before. I shut down the link as much as I could earlier. No offense but I really didn't want to feel you being with someone else. But I did feel you having a good time. Three times actually."

Tracy blushed furiously. "Okay, that's enough of that topic."

He laughed.

"Are you all right?" she asked him softly, reaching up fingertips to feather through his ebony hair.

Exhaling, he nodded. "I am. I am because it's the last thing to help us start our life together. You're safe and I'm relieved." He took her hand and they went into the living room.

"I spoke to my realtor, he's one of the higher-ranking members of Pacific. I've got him scouting out homes for us with nice views of the city and close in—my needs—and big yards suitable for dogs—your need. He's going to get us some listings together and we can start looking tomorrow. Is that all right?"

She warmed as her heart filled near to bursting with her love for him. "Thank you, Nick. I know you'll love Milton. He couldn't stay here though, he loves to run. So I'm going to ask Nina to babysit him until we can get a bigger place. At some point I need to get back up to Seattle to figure out what to do with my house and my store."

He looked at her, feeling the sadness at the mention of selling her business. "Baby, have you considered keeping it and hiring some other staff to run it for you?"

"I don't know. I can trust Charity, she's full-time anyway and I know she'd welcome the extra money. And there are a few of my staff that I could hire on full-time. I'd have to run the numbers to see what my profit margin would be. But what would I do here?"

"We just lost our accountant not too long ago. Didn't you say you did the accounts for Cascadia?"

"Yes, and I can help until you hire someone else on, but I'm not an office job kind of woman, Nick. In case you haven't noticed, I'm the facial piercing type. My hair is frequently odd colors and I like to come and go as I please. You can't do that unless you own a funky business like a record store or you help with the books when your brother is the Alpha."

"In case *you* hadn't noticed, your brother-in-law is the Alpha. Like Ben is going to care if your hair is what—blue? Pink? And that damned brow ring is growing on me. It's sexy. But you could open up a record store down here if you wanted. A second Spin the Black Circle. That could be good."

"I've thought about it. I need to do some research to see what's down here already. There aren't a whole lot of independent record stores anymore so if there are two or three in a city this size, that's already filling that niche."

"Take your time. Hell, be a woman of leisure if you want."

She laughed. "Well, thank you, but no. I like working, I just need it to be what I like. And eventually we'll have children and a flexible schedule will be a must." She froze at the look on his face. "You do want children, don't you?"

His eyes filled up with unshed tears. "Yes. Yes I do, and I was beginning to wonder if it would ever happen. But the thought of a little girl with your eyes and those freckles just makes me happy, baby."

She released the breath she'd been holding. "Oh good. I want them too. In a few years."

"We've got time. So now what we've tap-danced around it, what are you going to do about the joining?"

"What does *she* say?"

"What do you mean?"

Tracy looked at him, annoyed. "Nick, do I look slow to you? Of course you called her and told her what happened. What did she say?"

"Am I that transparent? I just wanted to talk to her, to let her know you were upset. It was nothing more than that."

"Oh yes, we mustn't let sweet Sarah get her fee-fees hurt. God knows how fragile she is. You know, she is an Alpha female, Nick. She can hang with the big dogs. She can certainly talk shit like one."

"Tracy, she really isn't like that. She was caught off-guard and she's really upset that you overheard her saying all of that about you. She doesn't want you to get the wrong idea and she desperately wants you to like her. It's important to her. Family is important to her."

"Uh-huh. So back to my question. What did she say about the joining?"

"She would be horrified if you didn't join the Pack because of what you overheard her say in what she termed today, *a moment of jealous lunacy.* She wants you to be a part of Pacific. You're my mate, that in and of itself is important to her. She's the Alpha female. But she's also my sister-in-law and she wants you to feel welcome. Lastly, she really wants to get to know you. She knows you're coming to a new city and will need new friends and a family to fill in for yours since you'll be a few hours away. She asked me to see if you'd give her another chance."

Now that she'd experienced the intensity of the anchor bond she understood Sarah's behavior a lot better. It still bothered her that Sarah had said the things she did, but what else could she do? There was no place for Nick in Cascadia. Lex wasn't just an Enforcer but *the* Enforcer. He was the bar that other Enforcers strove toward. And Nick was born to be Second in Pacific. Tracy was the youngest of six, she had the freedom to do what she wanted. And she wanted to be with Nick.

"I still don't like her. But I'll go tonight to see what she says to my face. I want this to work, Nick, I really do. Because I love you."

He smiled and she felt his relief.

"Now, I have a problem. You smell like another wolf, which makes me want to fuck that right out of you. In addition, you smell like my mate, which also makes me want to fuck you. You are deliciously sexy and each breath you take pushes those sweet nipples against your shirt, showing me those rings. Refer back to my previous proposed action."

"Why, Nick, would you care to retire to the bedroom to have wanton hot monkey love?"

He threw back his head and laughed. "No, baby. I want you to get those jeans off and bend over the arm of this couch right now. I feel the need to christen this room."

"Oh, my," she said faintly as she rose to obey.

Chapter Four

ဩ

Some hours later, Tracy and Nick drove up the pretty driveway of the Pacific Pack house. Tracy felt languid and satisfied. Nick had made love to her all afternoon long in every room and on every piece of furniture that would hold them up. She felt thoroughly taken care of and desired.

She snuck a look over at him and smiled. He had a bite mark on his neck that he hadn't bothered to try and hide. In fact, she suspected that he'd forgone a shirt with a collar to show it off. At one point her wolf had surfaced and she'd bitten him, hard, right as she came. Because the bite was from another wolf, it would be there for a while instead of healing within hours.

Happiness stole over her when she saw her parents' BMW and Cade's Mercedes along with the SUV they'd driven down in the day before. Her family was there! She suddenly felt the need to hug her mother.

Nick parked and turned to her. "Wow, look at you. You're brimming with joy. It's seeing your family here?"

She nodded. "That and the bite on your neck that you're showing off like a teenaged boy."

He laughed and kissed her quick but hard. "Baby, this mark is hot. You're hot. I've never had a bite before. Of course I want to show it off. Now come on, let's go inside."

Milton came tearing around the house to greet her, goofy grin and all, and she squealed in delight. "Hi, Milton! Oh, I missed you!" She got to her knees and hugged him. She turned and caught Nick's look of horror. "Nick, this is Milton. Milton, this is Nick." She smooched Milton's nose and went on seriously, "Nick's uptight but quite okay once you get to know him. I fear he is freaked out by your lack of a leg."

Nick smiled despite himself. How could he deny her a thing that clearly made her happy? Even if it was a three-legged dog. He bowed low. "I am pleased to meet you, Milton. Any dog of Tracy's is welcome in my Pack."

Milton looked him up and down and nodded, tongue hanging out the side of his mouth. He leaned forward and licked Nick's hand. Nick tried to pretend that it didn't touch him and Tracy tried not to fall over dead at the utter cuteness of her two bestest guys.

Nina came around the house with Haley and Chris, Sarah and Ben's children. "Hi, Stinky! I see your mom is here with your new dad. I'd make him buy me a pony if I were you."

The kids looked up at Nina, decided she was hilarious and laughed loudly as they spilled over to where Tracy and Nick were standing with Milton.

"Uncle Nick! You didn't tell us that Tracy had a dog!"

"I'm sorry, guys. A terrible oversight on my part that I will not repeat."

"Have you been playing with Milton?" Tracy asked Haley.

"Oh yeah, he's the funnest dog ever. Well, the only dog I've ever played with really. And he's great. He runs and gets the ball and it doesn't even bug him that he only has three legs and he gets the ball all gooey with his slobber and then Chris tries to gross me out with it but he's just a lame boy 'cause that doesn't gross me out at all." Haley had to stop to take a breath after that run-on sentence but the smile never left her face.

"Tell you what. When Nick and I move into our new house and Milton comes down to live with us, you can come and play with him any time your mom and dad say it's okay."

Nick reached out and squeezed her hand.

"Really? Cool!" The kids jumped around and Milton followed suit, barking.

"He's safe to leave out here? He won't hurt the children?" Nick asked as the kids ran into the side yard with Milton.

"He's a gentle soul. He would kill or die to protect them but he'd never hurt them."

He kissed her temple. "Thank you for making the kids feel welcome at our home."

She looked sideways at him, surprised. "You think you're the only person family is important to? Of course I wanted them to feel welcome. They're my niece and nephew now too and they seem like great kids."

Sarah was standing on the porch and Tracy looked up at her. Nina reached out to grab her arm.

"Can I talk to you a second?"

"Sure." Tracy turned to Nick. "I'll be up in a minute."

He caressed her cheek. "All right. I'll be waiting. I see that Gabe is here too, surrounded by females." He laughed and Tracy felt a stab of jealousy.

She and Nina walked down the yard a bit, out of hearing of the wolves on the porch. "What's up?"

"You tell me. I thought we'd hear from you today but nothing. I know you've been fucking like crazy, but what gives? I thought you were my Best Friend Forever?"

Tracy laughed and hugged Nina. "Just like Lucy and Ethel. You are my BFF, goofus. And we have been fucking like crazy. It is so totally like sexual crack! But we had a bit of trouble last night and then the tri-bond. It was so...intense. I didn't expect it to be so... I didn't expect to feel so deeply for Gabe. It scared me."

"Well, I know you're not blind so you must see that I'm just a bit in love with Cade. Not anywhere near what I feel for Lex, but a part of me yearns for Cade and I'm guessing it always will. Lex knows. Of course, he also knows that Cade and I would never do anything to hurt or betray him. It'll get easier to process over time, Stinky's mom. And you want to elaborate on the *trouble* from last night?"

Tracy told her about the overheard phone call and Nina looked back over her shoulder at Sarah, who winced slightly. "That blonde bitch had the nerve to talk shit about you to Nick? Oh uh-uh! You're coming back home with us right now!"

Tracy took Nina's arm, which had been gesticulating wildly, and laughed. "Nina, it's okay. Nick and I talked for a long time about it and worked through it. I believe him when he says he just wanted to share his happiness over the bond with his friend. I don't like that he called her his best friend, but I'm hoping that over time he'll think of me that way instead."

"And what about her?"

Lex came out onto the porch, sensing Nina's anger, and began to move toward them both.

"Shit. Listen, please let me work this out. Lex will just try and protect me and I need to do this on my own."

"What is going on?" Lex demanded curtly and over his shoulder, Tracy saw Cade come out onto the porch, followed by Gabe. Nick looked worried.

"Nothing! Sheesh, can't a girl share the juicy details of her bonding night with her best friend?"

Lex put his hands over his ears. "Never mind! Don't elaborate. Let's get this thing started before an incident happens."

Nina kissed Tracy's cheek softly. "I got your back, sister."

Tracy smiled. "Thanks, Nina. That means so much to me. I love you."

"Everything okay?" Cade called out as they approached the porch.

"Fine, fine. Just girl talk." She sent a look up to Nick, who exhaled and held out his hand.

"Before you go inside, Tracy, can you stand a bit more girl talk?" Sarah asked.

Nina touched her back and moved away, murmuring to Cade and Lex, and everyone walked inside.

Tracy leaned against the porch railing and Nick moved beside her, banding his arm about her waist.

"Tracy, I understand from Nick that you overheard some of the things I said to him on the phone this morning."

"When you talked smack about me? Told my mate you loved him? That conversation?"

Nick tensed up and Tracy told herself that if he didn't back her up, she'd walk off the property right then, mate or no.

Sarah sighed. "Yes, that one. I realize that it caused a fight between you two and led you to consider not joining Pacific to serve as Second with Nick. And I'm terribly sorry. What was said was said in a moment of high emotion. God, I'm so embarrassed. It was petty and small and I hope that we can get past it because Nick means a lot to me and you mean everything to him and you're family now. You'd also be one of my wolves. And it would break Ben's heart to know that my jealousy had broken the Pack this way."

"Nick, I need you to go inside and wait for me please."

"Tracy, I…"

She looked at him with one raised brow.

"All right. Tracy, I love you. I want you here with me, in my Pack, at my side." Nick kissed her and pulled back, tucking a wayward curl behind her ear.

"I love you too. I'll be in in a moment."

He looked back over his shoulder at her and left them alone on the porch.

Tracy turned around to Sarah. "Now that we're alone I just have a few things to say. First, I could not possibly care less if you like me or my eyebrow ring or how skinny I am. Certainly I would have preferred a warm welcome without fake smiles and pretending to like me in front of others. But whatever. The raw fact is that you had no business slagging me off to my mate. The wolf in me finds that very hard to get past. Nick is not yours. *Ben* is yours. Nick may be your anchor but he is my mate. Don't think to ever try and get around me to him again or there will be trouble.

"I will join Pacific. For Nick. As to whether I forgive you or not, only time will tell if what you did and said is an aberration. Now that I have an anchor, I understand your reaction a lot better. But actions are the proof, I don't put much stock in words. I'm going to pledge my fealty tonight but I want to tell you, alone out here, that you haven't earned it. I'm doing this for one reason only, because Nick asked me to and I love him. But make no mistake, Sarah, I will tear your fucking head off if you ever try it again. Alpha or not."

Sarah's face was red and her eyes narrowed. Tracy knew that part of Sarah's apology had been a front for Nick's benefit, but how much of it would only be clear over time. "Okay."

Tracy lowered her chin slightly, just enough to show deference and she was sure Nick relaxed from the place he'd been spying on them.

When they walked inside, she saw her parents and grandmother there with Nick's parents. She rushed over to her mother and let herself be comforted by her presence.

"Oh, sweet girl! A million congratulations on you both. Let me meet this boy."

Tracy held her hand out and Nick took it. "Mom and Dad, Grandma, this is Nick Lawrence. Nick, this is my mother Beth and my father, Henri Warden. And my grandmother Lia."

Nick bowed to her parents and took her mother's hand, kissing it and then her grandmother's. He shook her father's hand solemnly. "Mr. and Ms. Warden, Mrs. Warden, it's my honor to have you here in Pacific House and doubly so to have Tracy as my mate."

Her father looked Nick over carefully and slowly nodded. "Welcome to the family, son."

Cade came forward and shook Nick's hand and then Ben came up and there was a lot of sniffing and other status marker behavior that made Tracy look to Nina and roll her eyes.

"Oh, and Mom and Dad and Grandma," she reached out and grabbed Gabe's hand, the connection shocked her but she tried to hide it, "this is Gabe Murphy, my anchor."

Her grandmother looked closely at the two of them but smiled and shook his hand.

"Shall we perform the joining ceremony?" Ben called out and the room quieted.

Nick looked to Tracy, holding his breath until Tracy nodded.

Walking to the center of the room, Ben and Sarah stood facing Tracy and Nick. As her anchor, Gabe stood to the other side as well.

"Do you swear fealty to Pacific Pack and her wolves? Do you pledge your life to her well-being and your obedience to her Alphas?"

"I do."

"Then stand and be recognized Tracy Lawrence, Second and new Packmate."

There was applause and Tracy became a member of Pacific Pack.

A feast was awaiting them in the large dining room and soon Tracy began to relax and get to know her new family. The wolves from Pacific, for the most part anyway, seemed to be happy to have her there. She did notice the small, all-female contingent hovering around Gabe and pointedly ignoring her, but she tried not to let it bother her. Gabe was her anchor and hers on a level those skanks could never understand.

Gabe watched her all evening. The light shone off her skin and hair and she seemed to glow with her happiness. She was so beautiful and animated and he wanted to kick Nick's teeth in for having her. Tracy Warden should be his, damn it.

"So are you going to be around Portland a lot more now that you're her anchor?" one of the females who'd quite obviously been rubbing against him all night, asked him.

"Well, probably. I like it here. It's a nice change of pace and scenery from where I live in Virginia."

"So please explain her appeal. What is it? She's gawdawful, like Hot Topic exploded or something. Who pierces their face? A guy like Nick gets snatched up by her?"

Gabe heard the whispered discussion from behind him and turned slowly.

The other wolf continued, oblivious to Gabe's presence. "She thinks she's better because she comes from Cascadia. We'll see how it feels for her now that she's down here where every damned female in this room has had her mate."

"I think you'd best close that nasty mouth of yours," Gabe said in a low growl and the three wolves who'd been gossiping jumped.

"Uh, oh. What's it to you anyway?" one of the lesser wolves said, the light of too much alcohol and not enough brains in his eyes.

"Excuse me? Are you not speaking of your new Second in a derogatory fashion and now addressing me in that same disrespectful way?" Discipline at Pacific was sorely lacking, that much was clear.

Ben approached with Nick. "Is there a problem here?"

"We were just talking. We didn't mean anything by it!"

"What's going on, Gabe?" Nick asked.

Gabe looked to be sure Tracy wasn't nearby before he spoke. "Just some of your wolves shooting off about your mate."

Nick glared at the other wolves, who looked down, not bold enough to challenge their Enforcer.

Tracy, seeing the gathering of males with concerned faces, got up and went over. "What's going on?"

"Nothing, baby." Nick put his arm around her but she caught the looks the others were wearing.

"Okay. If you say so." She knew it was a lie but she didn't want to cause trouble. She just wanted to make the night a success.

Nick saw that and smiled at her, kissing her temple. "I like it when you're this easy."

Tracy laughed. "I'll show you even more easy later," she murmured into his ear.

"She isn't worthy of you, Nick! Why are you all bending over for her?" One of the females who'd been sending Tracy dirty looks all evening stepped forward.

"What? You jealous that I'm getting bent over and not you?" Tracy asked, moving forward and directly into the personal space of the other female.

Shelley, the redhead whose scent had been all over Nick's sheets, laughed. "She's got you there, Jo."

Tracy took the other woman's measure. There hadn't seemed to be any animosity and the redhead had been friendly and open toward her so she judged that she wasn't a threat. Interesting, that.

She cut her eyes back to the incredibly stupid blonde who was challenging her. It was lunacy. Tracy was Second in the Pack and came from a powerful line of wolves. She was clearly far more dominant and capable of tearing Blondie apart. More than that, mates were mates, it wasn't like jealousy would change the biological connection between her and Nick.

"I saw your little act out there on the porch," Blondie hissed. "You think you can just waltz in here and take Second?"

Tracy snorted and stepped in closer. She could feel Nick's tension and no small amount of arousal at her back. "Did you now? You sure are fascinated with me. What's your problem anyway?"

Ben touched her shoulder and she turned, growling, and he backed off. "Tracy, let's just calm down."

Nick pushed between his brother and Tracy, muscles tensed. "Don't touch her, Ben."

"She should calm down? What kind of Pack is this, anyway? A far lesser wolf disrespects her and she's the one who needs to calm down?" Gabe growled, tense from the sight of Ben's hand on Tracy's shoulder and Tracy's growl of defense. He stood at Nick's side, ready to defend them both if necessary.

Nick looked at Gabe and then back at Tracy and over to Ben. Everyone was still for a moment as Ben stood there, nose to nose with Nick.

Tracy sighed and turned back to Blondie. "You have a problem with me? Fine. It's a free country. But don't think to challenge me. You don't have the slightest hope of winning. And even if you could, you don't have a chance in hell with Nick. Sour grapes don't look good on you."

She turned and leaned into Nick's body. "Back off, babe. It's over now. I don't want you fighting with your brother," she murmured into his ear.

"We don't need this drama, Tracy. You're the new person here. You just need to understand that a new Pack member is slightly upsetting." Ben's tone was patronizing.

Suddenly Gabe was at her back and things began to really slide out of control. "Perhaps you can explain Pack governance to us then? A Second should allow herself to be disrespected because some female won't be fucking Nick anymore? And so Tracy is the one who brought the drama? Over there on the couch trying to make friends?"

"Perhaps you can explain why you're speaking for my brother's mate," Ben said with a growl.

"Perhaps you can all stop talking about me like I'm a chair!"

Nick was still holding her back and Cade and Lex had come over. Blondie smirked.

"Control your mate, Nick," Sarah said and Tracy's eyebrows shot up.

"What? What did she just say?" Cade growled and Nina was there, trying to calm him down.

And in the midst of the chaos, a blur of movement came from the left. Tracy, wedged between Gabe and Nick, couldn't move and it knocked her down, but she was up and on top of Blondie in milliseconds, teeth bared.

"Stand down!" Ben yelled.

"Why should she?" Gabe demanded.

"If she'd just kept calm none of this would have happened!" Ben yelled back.

"This is not her fault!" Nick growled.

"I should kill you for that," Tracy growled at blondie, who finally had the good sense to see just how outmatched she was and trembled beneath Tracy's grip.

"I said, stand down." It was then that the full impact of how ill-suited Ben was to lead the Pack hit Tracy. She had zero compunction to obey his command like she would have with Cade. If Cade had yelled an order like that she would have had no other choice but to obey. Pacific was a Pack rotting from the inside because it had an Alpha who wasn't capable of leading. A sinking feeling took hold in Tracy's gut.

Still, she had to deal with the situation at hand. So she continued to ignore Ben and kept focused on the women beneath her. "What do you say, Blondie? Should I rip your empty little head off for jumping me blind like a coward?" Tracy's face was up close to the other woman's, just barely holding back her wolf. But she did let it show in her eyes so Blondie would know just how close she was to real trouble.

Dimly she heard Ben move in her direction and Nick's answering move to stop him. Gabe stayed in her peripheral vision, at the ready if he was needed. "He's not going to save you, you know. Have you decided what you're going to do yet?" Tracy's voice was the barest of sounds but it registered.

"I…I apologize. Please, mercy. I was wrong to have attacked you blind. I yield."

Tracy let go and stood up, turning her back on Blondie to let her know just how little she feared her. "You bet you do." She turned her gaze on Ben. "I do not stand down when I've been challenged." And it wasn't Ben's place to stop her in that situation either, she'd been attacked and it was well within her rights to answer the challenge, even to the death. But she didn't say that, not wanting to hurt Nick or cause any more trouble.

"You'll do what I say you will." Ben raised his chin.

Tracy moved forward and there was a general shuffling of wolves as people moved to intervene. She stopped when she'd reached Ben and Sarah. "You'd have to have the authority to do that." Her voice was low but deadly. She wouldn't escalate but she wouldn't cow to an unreasonable threat to her either.

"Clear out!" Sarah ordered and most of the wolves complied but for Nick, Cade, Lex and Nina and their assorted parents. Gabe stayed as well.

"You have been insubordinate, Tracy. You've brought trouble into this Pack."

"Bullshit. You can't control your Pack and you're looking to blame me for it. I didn't do anything wrong. Your wolf—an unranked wolf—jumped me blind. That's an unacceptable breach of discipline. No Pack would frown on me defending myself, which is what I did. By rights I could have killed her for it, I didn't even blood her."

Ben pushed her and, shocked, she froze for a moment until she shoved him back. It occurred to her then that she could take him in a challenge. Her wolf was incensed and she did her best to rein it in.

"What is wrong with you?" Nick demanded of his brother in a growl. He pushed against Ben, his eyes had begun to get that otherworldly blue that she knew signaled his wolf trying to surface to defend her. His hands were around Ben's throat, squeezing, Ben was desperately clawing at him to get him to let go. "You just shoved my mate!"

"Nick and Ben! Stop it this instant!" Chuck Lawrence, the former Alpha and their father, stepped in, pulling Nick back. "Ben, this is insane! This is your brother's mate, a Second in your Pack. You just put your hands on her!"

"Don't do it again," Gabe said in a growl.

"And what the fuck is that all about anyway?" Sarah demanded. "Why is he speaking for your mate, Nick? Have you asked yourself that question? Just what is between them?"

"Oh you'd love that, wouldn't you? Jesus, what kind of Alpha throws blood in the water? What's *your* agenda, Sarah?" Tracy was outraged. And upset. The whole evening was a clusterfuck.

"Tri-mate bond."

Everyone got quiet and looked at Lia, Tracy's grandmother.

"What? What did you just say?" Nick looked at her, eyes wide.

"It's the tri-mate bond. Surely I'm not the only one who can see it?"

"The tri-mate bond is a fairy tale." Gabe's voice was flat as he said it but his heart raced at the thought.

"So are werewolves." Ben and Nick's mother said this kindly but firmly. "And it does happen. Not often, but once every generation or so. I can't believe I didn't see it until now."

"What makes you think it's a tri-mate bond?" Tracy asked, stung by Gabe's fairy tale comment but not sure why.

"It isn't real!" Nick's voice was urgent and he grabbed Tracy's hand.

"Mrs. Warden, I'm Tracy's anchor, nothing more. Nick is her mate." Gabe struggled for calm.

"You know that's a lie." Lia's voice was calm and sure.

"Enough! What the heck makes you think so?" Tracy's frustration was clear as she chewed her bottom lip. Her grandmother was up on that kind of stuff. She was an elder and knew the old ways and all of the metaphysical stuff that always made Tracy tune out. Cade always listened to it though, and one look at his face had Tracy more than a little freaked out.

"You three need to work this out in private." Nick's mother turned to Tracy. "Honey, I'm sorry about all that happened here tonight. There's an awful lot of Alpha in one small space. I'd like to ask that you give us another chance after you, Nick and Gabe work all of this through."

"What is going on?" Nina murmured to Lex.

"I'll explain later."

"You need to control your mate!" Sarah said around Ben.

"And you need to shut the fuck up! Get over it already, Sarah. You can't have them both. Nick is my mate. I'm not giving him up." Tracy wanted to smack the other woman. Nothing worse than a phony.

"You think he'd choose you over me?"

Fury roared through her. The very idea that anyone would challenge her for Nick filled her with murderous rage. "I think he has already, Sarah. But let me give him another chance." Tracy turned to Nick. "I know this night has been chaotic and upsetting so I'm giving you a chance here to walk away. If this tri-mate bond stuff is true, we're in for a bumpy ride. I love you enough to set you free. Supposedly there's some kind of spell that can sever the bond. We can investigate if that's what you want. But I can't have this up in the air. You need to choose and be clear about it." Tracy loved him so much she ached with it. But she loved him so much that she never wanted him to be with her with another woman in his heart either.

"There's no choice, Tracy. I made my choice in that maze. You're my mate. Period. I'm deeply ashamed of my brother, his mate and this Pack right now." He turned to Sarah. "I don't know what to say to you, Sarah. I've considered you my best friend all these years and now it feels like a lie. You've changed and I can't believe I haven't noticed. And Ben, this whole mess tonight was you. Your lack of leadership when it counted. And now it's yours to clean up. If you ever touch my mate again in anger, I'll kill you."

Ben stepped forward and the males in the room all started growling. Tracy sent a look to Nina, who appeared ready to tear Sarah's head off herself.

"I'm your Alpha, Nick. And your brother. Be careful how far you push my largesse."

"No, Ben. You should be careful. Because we both know that I could take you if I chose."

"Nick!" Sarah cried out and tried to get to him but Tracy stood forward and narrowed her eyes.

"What did I tell you about trying to get around me to him?"

Sarah halted, her eyes unsure.

"Enough! Ben, stand down! You'll not tear this Pack apart like this!" Nick's father shook his head before looking at Nick. "And you! Nick, don't say something you can't take back. I know this night has been upsetting and you have reason to be angry. But go home. Take Tracy and Gabe and deal with the tri-mate bond issue. Then we'll all deal with this mess."

"Good idea." Cade unclenched his hands and rolled his head on his neck to loosen up.

Tracy took Nick's hand. "Come on, babe. Let's go before this gets any worse. Please." She didn't want to beg but she would. She was seriously concerned about what would happen if they stayed any longer.

"This isn't over, Ben. There's an accounting to be had." Nick turned, put an arm around Tracy, looked at Gabe and gestured toward the door with a jerk of his head.

The Cascadia wolves in attendance caught up with them in the driveway.

"Tracy, I don't want to leave you here in the midst of this mess," Lex said, looking very agitated. Nina was stroking her hands down his back, trying to calm him down.

"I appreciate that you care about your sister's well-being, Lex, but she's my mate. I'll see to her safety. You should all probably go, though. Your status is going to be a point of contention and I don't want any of you to be insulted or threatened."

"Oh god, can we just go home? Seriously, I am going to fall over in about five minutes. Nina, will you keep Milton for a while? I'm sorry to do this and I miss him but I don't have a place to put him and…" Tracy's voice broke and Nina hugged her tight, assuring her she'd take care of the dog and ease back on the tofu corn dogs too.

Tracy's adrenaline was going to crash, she felt emotionally exhausted. She knew her grandmother was right. Knew why she'd been so intensely affected by Gabe when they bonded earlier. He wasn't her anchor, he was her mate. And that comforted her and filled her with joy at the same time as it scared the hell out of her. The ramifications of dealing with two very alpha werewolves and different Pack ranks and whatever the hell was going on in Pacific were mind-boggling.

Gabe had been trying very hard not to step into Nick's place but damn it all, could they not see how Tracy needed to get out of there? "Tracy, get in the car. Nick, I'll meet you at your apartment. Cade, Lex, everyone, Nick is right and I'm in an odd position here but still, there is an Alpha overload and it's bound to complicate things further."

He said all of it as he helped Tracy into the car and strode back toward his rental.

The Wardens all agreed, with the reminder that if there was trouble to call them for help. Lia spoke quietly to Tracy before she turned and walked with the rest of the family to their cars.

The drive back to the apartment was quiet but Nick's hand was on her thigh when he wasn't shifting gears.

He helped her out of the car and she let him take care of her, both of them needing that. Gabe was waiting near the elevators.

* * * * *

Once inside the apartment Tracy kicked off her shoes and went to the couch, where she collapsed. Nick handed her a drink and she thanked him.

Looking up at Gabe, emotion rushed through her and she accepted it. She'd tried to pretend it was just the anchor bond but the truth was, she knew even then. Since the first moment he'd touched her she'd been falling into him and when he'd come inside her that morning she was lost. Her heart belonged to Gabe as much as it belonged to Nick.

"Let's cut to the issue, shall we?" Her voice wasn't as steady as she'd wanted it to be but she was in the room with two incredibly attractive males who, unless she was totally wrong, belonged to her. "My grandmother is never wrong about this stuff. And your mother, Nick, seemed to agree."

Nodding with a sigh, Nick sat next to her and Gabe across from them on the low table.

"Gabe, you seem to be exhibiting behavior which would indicate you feel mated to Tracy." Nick said all of this dryly.

"Well, yes. It's been since this morning. Since the bonding. It was there before, the attraction, but this *need* is there now. And I have feelings of protection and kinship to you as well." Gabe said this with a slight shrug of his shoulders.

That got her attention. *Well.*

"Let's go over this from the beginning. I don't believe I have all the facts about the tri-mate bond. Can you tell me everything you know?" Gabe had been schooled about werewolf culture and history, but something like the tri-mate bond was so rare that it wasn't a common topic of discussion.

"Simply put, the tri-mate bond happens when the people in the tri-bond seal a mating instead of just an anchoring. As you're aware, the tri-bond anchors the female mate to another wolf. In a sense it's like the third leg on a stool. But aside from an emotional closeness there's not an actual *mate* bond. But every great once in a while, during the tri-bond the female becomes mated to the third wolf—to the person she's supposed to be anchored by. And the twinned mate bond becomes a mate bond of three. If I'm remembering correctly it happens in rare situations when the combination of males could be interchangeable. By that, I mean that either male could be a mate to the female. The odds are astronomical, really." Tracy was pleased that she'd listened to her grandma more than she thought she had.

Gabe nodded and moved forward enough that his leg just barely touched Tracy's. "I was drawn to you, which is a sign. You're an exceptional woman. But not my usual type by a long shot." He saw the wince and touched the back of Tracy's hand. "And I don't mean that in a bad way."

"I don't know anyone that this has ever happened to. The accounts do say it happens almost exclusively to Alpha wolves and their mates so I didn't think about it."

Tracy chewed on her bottom lip and decided to say it anyway. "Well, babe, I have news for you, you're far more of an Alpha than your brother is. And Gabe is a very dominant wolf too. If either of you had your own Pack, you could easily be the Alpha."

Nick scrubbed hands over his face. "I don't want this, you know."

Tracy turned to him and cradled his face in her hands. "I'm sorry. For this mess tonight with your Pack. And well, how do we deal with this for you? If it is the tri-mate bond, it's not like we can will it away. When my grandmother spoke to me just before we left, she told me the stories of spells that could terminate the bond were all untrue. A wolf can choose not to seal the bond. Walk away and not look back. Eventually, they'd find another mate out there, most likely. But once the bond is sealed, it's sealed. I wish I could make this better for you. You must be so sorry you met me."

Nick's breath froze. After all of the upheaval in her life, having to leave her city, Pack, business and home behind, the way his family treated her that night—after all of that she actually worried about him and his feelings? He leaned into her palm. "Oh baby, never that. You're a joy to me. Finding you is something I'd never regret. As for the tri-mate bond? Tracy, it is what it is. I can't change it. Do I want to share you? No. No, I don't. But Gabe is every bit as much your mate as I am. Without you, he'll never find real happiness. He won't be able to be with any other females now that you've sealed the bond. How could I wish him such emptiness? And how could I even begin to ask you to live without your mate? And he is your mate as much as I am. And because of that, he's mine too. It's the only way I can explain why I don't want to kill him right now."

"How do you feel about me?" Gabe asked Tracy.

"I…" She was afraid to say it out loud. She didn't want to hurt Nick but she could see that Gabe needed the words. "This morning was so intense. Nick and I had a terrible fight earlier and then made up and I felt complete, you know? But I could also feel the yawning depths of the lack of an anchor. I was feeling edgy and way less in control than I usually am. And then you came in." She held on to Nick's hand and reached out with her free hand to Gabe. His fingers—warm and strong— received and wrapped around hers.

"The bonding was so profound, so amazing and deep. I kept telling myself that I was just surprised because I hadn't been bonded to an anchor before. I knew how Nina felt about

Cade and I understood Sarah a lot more than I had earlier."
She rolled her eyes. "And that's a topic for later, by the way.
But after you left, I felt your absence so strongly. I was jealous
when I saw those females around you. And then tonight when
you defended me and Nick at his side it felt *right*. It feels like
you're mine like Nick is mine."

Gabe's eyes were warm and his lips hitched at one corner
into a sexy smile. "Thank god I'm not alone."

Nick held out his hand to Gabe, who took it, and a circuit
was created then. Each of the tri-mate bond physically
connected and electric heat careened through them, hot
enough to bring a gasp from their lips. A warm wind
disturbed Tracy's hair. Her wolf rolled within her, pushing
against her humanity and attempting to touch Gabe's and
Nick's wolves as well.

"Yeah. Uh, wow." Nick's voice was awed as the emotion
and magic of the moment rolled through the room. "I think
that if there was any doubt before, it's gone now."

Tracy nodded mutely as waves of gooseflesh broke
through her over and over. The pleasure of being there,
touching both of them, was almost too much to bear.

"Not to be indelicate but I'd really like to fuck you right
now, Tracy," Gabe whispered hoarsely.

Again, all she could do was nod. But she looked to Nick.
"How are we going to do this so that everyone is okay?"

"Right now let's just get naked and we'll work from
there." Nick stood and began to unbutton his shirt.

Tracy stood up on shaky legs and undid the side zipper
on her pants while Gabe's hands went to her sweater and
pulled it up and off while Nick shoved her pants down her
legs.

"Holy shit, how did I miss this tattoo on your back?"
Gabe turned her around and leaned down. She looked back at
him over her shoulder.

"I don't think you got back there."

"Hmm. Well, that needs to be remedied. Has anyone been back there, baby?" Nick murmured, his lips against that space where neck meets shoulder.

She couldn't think straight with both of them so near! Both men were shirtless and she was naked except for her panties. The heat of their bodies blanketed her and intoxicated her, lulling her senses in an erotic stew.

"I...uh...what was the question?" Tracy swayed a bit, drunk on the heady emotions in the room created by the three of them.

Gabe laughed just before he dragged a tongue up her spine.

Tracy reached around, grabbed the waist of his pants and clumsily but effectively undid them and moved to touch Nick and do the same.

She fell to her knees and rubbed her cheek across Nick's cock. She loved the feel of him there, soft and hard all at once. Loved it when his hands on her shoulders tightened and pulled her closer.

Looking up at him, she saw how dark his eyes had gotten. His lips were parted and her clit throbbed when his tongue came out to sweep across his bottom lip.

"That's a fine start. Don't let me stop you now," Nick murmured.

Gabe standing close behind her, she took Nick into her mouth. Slowly. Her tongue circled the head and what she'd learned was his sweet spot just beneath the slit. His taste burst over her, through her, and she took him back as far as she could and pulled back again.

She let out a sound of surprised pleasure when Gabe grabbed her hair and began to guide her movements.

"Yessss," Nick hissed. His thumbs moved up and stroked over the line of her throat, leaving her skin tingling in their wake. Leaving her wanting more of him. Gabe's hands in her hair, his control of her movements, sizzled her neural pathways leading to her nipples and pussy. She was so wet she could feel it on her thighs.

"Wait. I want to fuck you while you do this." Gabe pulled her head back and she looked up at Nick, who blinked slowly and nodded.

She took Nick's hand and he drew her toward the bedroom, her other hand in Gabe's. The whole scene felt utterly unreal and she wasn't sure she'd spoken in several minutes. She certainly knew she hadn't formed a coherent thought since Gabe had bent to look at the tattoo on her back. And who was a lucky girl? Sandwiched between two sexy, handsome, virile and powerful males the way she was made her lightheaded and giddy. *Wait 'til she told Nina!*

Nick lay on the bed and she scrambled over him.

"Hands and knees, Tracy. I want to look at that beautiful tattoo and watch you suck his cock."

She shivered in anticipation. There'd been hints earlier that Gabe was dominant, but clearly he wasn't holding back anymore. Positioning herself over Nick, she bent down and licked up the length of him before pulling him inside again.

Her moan of pleasure reverberated around Nick's cock when Gabe spread her thighs wider and dragged fingertips up the inside of her thighs.

"So soft. And, oh," he chuckled darkly when his fingers found her wet and swollen, circling around her clit and teasing slowly around her gate.

Her whimper of entreaty changed to a hum of satisfaction as he put the head of his cock where his fingers had been and began to push into her pussy. "Damn it, the way your pussy feels around me, I'm not sure that I've ever felt anything so good."

"Yeah, hot and tight and wet. The way she squirms when you bump over her sweet spot...makes my balls crawl up into my gut." Nick's voice was low and slightly out of breath as the two men locked eyes over Tracy's body. And in that glance, so much passed. A connection and a bit of chemistry too. They'd share this woman forever and in doing so, they'd be together as well. Gabe would be lying if he denied the thought didn't hold some appeal to him.

Tracy made a sound of disapproval when Gabe stopped moving. She squirmed back against him, tightening around him.

His palm landed soundly against the creamy flesh of her ass, leaving a red palmprint and a sting. "Pretty Tracy, we'll do this on my and Nick's schedule. I promise to make it worth your while." The sound trickled from his throat, part growl, part hoarse whisper. Impossibly sexy.

"Mmmm, tag-team fucking? I like that," Nick agreed and Tracy had to close her eyes as they both thrust into her body at the same time, filling her body and soul. Nick's hands in her hair were firm but gentle and Gabe leaned down to lay kisses at the back of her neck while one hand played against her clit and the other slowly rolled and pulled her nipple.

Each stroke of his fingers, each whispered word pulled her deeper and deeper into the maelstrom of emotion and pleasure the three of them created. It was overwhelming and yet, she felt like she could see it all with crystal clarity. The hands on her body, the lips at her neck, the crooned words from Nick and Gabe wove a spell around her, binding her to them. How could anything in the universe compare to feeling so cherished? So sexy and desired that she felt like a goddess. Sure she'd felt sexy in her life before, but this was different. These men believed she was everything and in that belief, she was. They all were. It was magic and beautiful.

Gabe looked down at her as she pressed that sweet little ass back against him to get more of his cock. God she was amazing. So gorgeous and sexy and smart. And so damned strong! When she'd jumped back on top of that bitch who'd knocked her down, teeth bared, voice a low threatening growl, he'd nearly pushed her back and taken her against the carpet in front of that crowd of people. Nothing in the universe was as sexy as his woman in full battle mode.

Her tattoo nearly glowed in the low light as she sweated with exertion. The scent of her desire rose and wove around his senses nearly as effectively as the way she felt wrapped around his cock.

Leaning forward, he watched her take Nick's cock into her mouth over and over and his own throbbed in anticipation. What a firecracker she was. So fucking hot and sexy that all she had to do was walk by and it made him hard. And it appeared she was amenable to submitting to him as well. He and Nick would have to work around each other, as much as Gabe was a dominant wolf, he was a sexually dominant male and there'd need to be a bit of negotiation to make it work for everyone.

"Deeper, that's right, baby. Yeah, oh yeah, right there," Nick mumbled softly, guiding her head. Her mouth was heaven over his cock. He loved the way he slipped in a bit deeper each time Gabe thrust into her, loved watching the sway of those delicious breasts. Her eyes looked straight into his, right into his soul, and he gave way to her, gave her every bit of himself.

He couldn't believe that he'd thought he'd been in love with Sarah. What he felt now for Tracy—what he'd felt since the moment he'd unleashed his semen deep inside her body was so intense and powerful that what he'd felt for Sarah was a pale imitation. This was his woman, his mate and he adored every inch of her, most notably the part sucking his cock at the moment, but the mischievous glint in those eyes too, the way her hair felt between his fingers, the curve of her back leading to where their mate was fucking into her.

When her fingertips pressed against his perineum he groaned and orgasm—just dancing out of reach—descended over him. Arching up into her body, he felt every nerve ending explode with endorphins until he was so wrung out that he couldn't hold himself up anymore and fell back to the bed.

"Thank you, baby. I love you. So very much." He combed fingers through her hair and she smiled at him, murmured that she loved him too before kissing the head of his cock. Turning her head, she laid it against his thigh and opened herself more to Gabe's invading cock.

Gabe smiled at Nick and began to fuck her with abandon. Her moans and mewls of pleasure rose in the air with the sounds of wet flesh meeting and his own grunts. Bringing thumb and forefinger together, he plumped them around her slippery, hard clit. Over and over, delighting in the way her thighs began to tremble and her moans became more desperate and breathy.

"Do you want to come, Tracy?"

"Yes!"

He laughed and flicked the tip of his finger over her clit with an insistent rhythm that matched his strokes into her pussy. The fluttering and clenching of the walls of her pussy signaled her impending climax and he knew it wouldn't be long after she came that he followed.

Her body seized and tightened as a pretty pink flush worked up her flesh. She cried out as orgasm flowed through her and she came around Gabe's cock. It seemed to last forever, each time she thought she was done, another wave would buffet her until she heard Gabe's groan and felt the jerk of his cock as he came deep inside her.

"Damn it, you're so sweet," he murmured as he flopped to the side and he kissed her when he and Nick pulled her up between them.

"Sweet? I just had a three-way with two alpha wolves! What's sweet about that?"

Nick laughed at her indignation and bent to kiss her nose. "I think he means sweet, like dark chocolate is sweet. Sinful and good but with a bite."

She crooked up a smile. "Oooh, good save."

"Why does he get the credit? I'm the one who said it!"

"Sure, but I said it better."

Tracy laughed at them. "We're going to need a bigger bed."

"And a house for your three-legged dog." Gabe was quite charmed by Milton and he'd seen Tracy's entire being light up when she'd seen him.

"Yeah. That's the least of our problems right now." Nick sighed.

Tracy tsked. "You're right. Because well, if you must know, no one has gone down on me. I'm a growing girl, I need it."

Gabe threw his head back and laughed. How long had it been since he'd felt so damned happy? Not in a very long time, if ever. And he'd certainly never felt the sense of family that he had right then.

"Well then, my love, let's remedy that. Can't neglect a growing girl, now can we?" He moved to kneel between her thighs and looked up the line of her body. So long and lean and pretty. Athletic and feminine, soft where she was supposed to be.

Her pussy was gorgeous and he traced the furl there, glistening and wet. "Why isn't this pierced?" He flicked a fingertip over her clit for emphasis.

Her breath caught. "It heals, or so I've been told. The nipples stay and the ears and eyebrow, because the rings have a core of silver that keeps my body from healing and pushing out the piercings but doesn't harm me. I'm not wild about putting that kind of thing near my clit. Damned werewolf super healing," she laughed.

"Good, because I don't want anyone else here looking at my pretty pussy. The idea of any other men here between your thighs makes me irritated." He moved his face closer and pulled at the hood with the tip of his tongue.

"I can't remember them anymore." And she wasn't lying. How could anything else compare?

It was Nick's turn to laugh as he moved to kiss her long and slow. His lips tasted her like she was something excruciatingly rare and delicious. Her hands were in his hair, holding his head to her.

He kissed like a man who viewed kissing as part of the lovemaking process. He didn't just do it to get to the fucking. Nick Lawrence was a connoisseur of the kiss. Deliberate little nips of his teeth followed by flicks of his tongue to soothe the sting. His tongue seduced its way into her mouth, slid along hers in a sinuous dance, making her breathless and wanting more of him. Needing more of his taste as it mixed with Gabe's.

Her hand wrapped around his cock and her other found Gabe's head.

Gabe loved oral sex. He loved to bring his partner pleasure in such an intimate way, loved to feel the changes in her body as her desire increased and she drew closer to coming. Each woman tasted a bit different but this one was so sweet that he knew he was already far past addicted. More than that, the wolf in him reacted to his own taste there. He needed her, she was an integral part of him now and he craved her touch, craved her voice and the cries of pleasure he brought her. Her taste would lie on his tongue until he died and he liked that very much.

So slick and responsive, her hips rolled up as he slid two fingers into her and hooked them. He'd found her sweet spot earlier that day and smiled against her flesh as he found it again and she jumped with a gasp that Nick eagerly swallowed.

His woman was not shy sexually. She knew what she wanted and she pressed herself greedily as he ate at her pussy. He loved it that she arched up when he moved his face from side to side quickly against her clit.

Rolling his eyes up, he watched as Nick laved over those freckles and down to her nipples, taking one and then the other into his mouth. It must be something about the bond because he couldn't imagine watching any male touching his mate like that and not killing him. But far from jealous rage, he loved watching Nick touch her.

Gabe watched her as he drew slick fingers down to the star of her rear passage and stroked over it. Her eyes opened and she instinctively tried to close her legs against him but his shoulders held her wide open to him.

"Shhh. If you don't like it I'll stop. I'd never hurt you or force you to do anything. But I would like both Nick and I to fuck you at the same time. Let me stretch you. It won't be tonight." Gabe waited until she relaxed. Slowly, the fingers stroking over her anus gave more pressure until he slowly entered just a little bit.

Holy shit, she was so tight. If her reaction to his first touches hadn't showed her as a newcomer to anal sex, the way she felt would have been a sure sign. He made a mental note to investigate some toys for her as he continued to lap at her flesh, devouring the sounds she made as much as he did her honey.

Nick kissed his way down her belly and Tracy thought she'd come on the spot as his tongue joined Gabe's.

"Oh my word..." she gasped. "Yes, please yes."

Her entire body began to tremble. Nick's palms burned into the skin of her inner thighs where he held her. Two tongues on her pussy, two fingers deep in her pussy and one tickling her ass, it was too much and for the first time she screamed as she came, unable not to.

Still, she wasn't too boneless to miss the brush of lips between Gabe and Nick when they moved away from her pussy. "Wow. That was really hot and I'd order you to do it again if I was anything other than a puddle of warm satiated goo."

Nick chuckled, surprised as much as she'd been but it had seemed natural to brush his lips over Gabe's. After all, they'd both been there going down on her at the same time.

Spooning into each other, they fell into a sleepy silence, muscles jumping and endorphins floating.

* * * * *

Gabe nestled his face into Tracy's neck, letting her scent wash through him, calming and relaxing him. He was utterly contented and he realized with a bit of a start that it was the first moment of such complete happiness and comfort he'd experienced in nearly thirty years.

All his life he'd felt different. As a kid growing up in the housing projects in Boston, his mother had made him stay inside to protect him from the violence of their world. Stuck inside, he turned to books.

He got a scholarship to a private high school and had excelled, getting a full ride to Yale. New Haven hadn't been so very different from his housing projects although, certainly the campus was a walled universe apart from the impoverished world just outside.

He got good grades and rarely went out those first years. He found it difficult to relate to anyone, as he always had. His mother hadn't even finished the ninth grade and his father had been on disability for most of Gabe's life due to a workplace accident that had broken his back. But suddenly he'd been surrounded by people who drove luxury cars and didn't have to sell plasma to pay for food. There were other students who'd come from impoverished backgrounds and Gabe had always figured if they all didn't have to work two jobs and study their asses off to keep their scholarships they might have hung out more.

Still, after a while he dated and had a wide circle of acquaintances, and the rare close friend. He'd never had trouble attracting women. He did have trouble keeping them once they'd progressed to the point where he wanted to open up the relationship to some of the sexual flavors he loved.

By the time he got into Harvard Law, he knew what he wanted to do and had a well-defined plan to get there. His father had died the year before and his mother had moved to upstate New York to live with his aunt. He was pretty much alone when Gavin Moore attacked him in a drunken rage.

Tim Moore, Gavin's dad and the Mediator for the National Pack for forty years, came to him in the hospital. From what Gabe learned later, the man had sat outside his room the day and a half it took him to recover from the attack.

Tim made his pitch. In exchange for Gabe keeping quiet about the attack, he'd be brought into the National Pack. Moreover, Tim would mentor him and the Pack would pay his tuition. Gabe had jumped at the chance. And he hadn't looked back.

Tim had been like a father to him. Not surprising really, since Gavin was a lazy, worthless asshat. Such indolence and a sense of entitlement—it drove Gabe nuts. But still, even though he'd shared holidays with the Moores, he'd never felt like one of them.

He was glad his mother lived long enough to see him graduate from Harvard. He'd bought her and his aunt a house and had taken good care of her those last years. But the hard life she'd lived up to that point had taken its toll and her diabetes and emphysema had both gone poorly treated for so long that even the best doctors money could buy had only been able to prolong her life for another ten years.

This woman and the man beside her were his now. His in a way that nothing had ever been before, and he would do anything to protect them both. Starting with finding out what the fuck was behind the odd way Ben and Sarah had acted earlier.

* * * * *

Nick's heart pounded beneath Tracy's hand, draped over his chest. A lazy smile touched his lips as she traced a heart there. He loved that sense of whimsy, it brought much-needed levity into his life. Even before the insanity of the evening at the Pack house, he'd known his life was too serious.

He moved into Tracy's body, feeling the cool steel of her nipple rings against his back. Her sweet little nipples were always hard, he most definitely liked that.

There'd been dozens of women that year alone. Each encounter had been satisfying physically but not emotionally. He'd told himself that he didn't need it, that emotional connection was for suckers. Besides, he'd had his friendships with Sarah and Josh, the Third in Pacific.

But as he lay there, he realized that he'd been lonely for the kind of connection he'd felt since he first bonded with Tracy. He not only loved her and was mated to her and to Gabe, but he felt a deep kinship with her. Whole where he'd felt empty.

All his life he'd purposely held himself back in the shadow so that Ben could excel. And most of the time Nick had been okay with that. He really hadn't wanted the pressure of being Alpha. It was a public, people-oriented position and as Enforcer, Nick had the kind of privacy and quiet that Ben could only dream of. The Pack house was constantly full of people and that would have driven him nuts.

At the same time, he knew something, something that his father and Ben knew too. Nick was far more qualified to be Alpha than Ben was. Nick was smarter and stronger and quicker. Just because Ben was older didn't mean he was automatically Alpha. And yet, Nick hadn't wanted to challenge or embarrass his brother. He loved Ben and Sarah and his niece and nephew.

Still, he was really thrown for a loop over Ben's and Sarah's behavior. That first night, when he'd taken Tracy to meet them, Ben had been a bit hesitant about his endorsement of Tracy, although he'd been pleasant enough to her face. And Sarah, well, he'd allowed her to convince him that it was just silly jealousy but clearly it was far more than that. He felt sick at making Tracy so upset with that phone call when she'd been right about Sarah's attitude.

"Hey, you were all warm and relaxed but you're all tensed up now." Tracy kissed his shoulder and he turned over to face her. "You want to talk about it?"

"You're far too distracting there naked and delicious and smelling like sex. Let's clean up and meet in the living room in a few minutes. I'll make some tea and we'll hash this situation with Pacific out."

Tracy sat up and climbed over him and sent them both a look back over her shoulder. "If you say so. But I might be lonely in there all by myself." And swayed her naked ass right into the connecting bath.

Gabe looked at Nick and they both laughed and got up to follow.

* * * * *

An hour later they stumbled into the kitchen and rustled up some tea and sandwiches for the discussion. Each one of them moved around each other with a kind of ease and rhythm that you don't get until you've known a person for some time.

Already their scents had begun to marry, to mix into one unique scent that would brand their sealed tri-mate bond. It teased Tracy's senses even as it warmed her insides.

Settling into the living room, Tracy sat in the big club chair near the fireplace and tucked her feet under her while she drank her tea.

"You wanna tell me what the hell happened tonight? I mean, is it normal behavior for the Pack to be so wild when you get a new member?"

Nick sighed heavily and leaned his head back against the couch. "We don't get new members very often but it's never been like this. I'm still totally shocked. Jo, the wolf who attacked you, she's not…she's not prone to attacking anyone. I don't understand."

"Let me guess, blondie, Jo, whatever-the-fuck, she's a friend of Sarah's."

Nick took a deep breath and nodded. "Jesus, you don't think?"

"That your bitchy, precious Sarah planned to try and fuck me over from the first moment she heard of me and enlisted that low-rent skank to try and start shit?"

Gabe burst out laughing and then sobered, wiping the tears from his eyes. He got up and moved to Tracy, kissing her and sitting back down. "Darling, you really must learn to express yourself better. Don't hold back."

Nick rubbed the bridge of his nose and smiled. "You think her apology was a fake?" He held up his hand. "No, don't answer that. I know it was. I'm sorry. You were right. I don't know how I could have been so wrong about her."

Tracy got out of the chair and came to kneel before Nick. She cradled his head between her hands. "Nick, you've known her all these years and she used that to manipulate you. I'd be lying if I said I was happy that you called her the way you did, but I understand why you did it. And she betrayed that."

He kissed the tip of her nose. "Thank you, baby. But I have a hard time believing that that entire thing tonight was out of simple jealousy that you are my mate."

"I'm with you on that, Nick. That scene tonight was way more complicated than mere jealousy. And in any case, Ben was agitated about something and it wasn't just a room full of alphas." Gabe had been around a lot of wolves with things to hide for the last twenty years and he was sure that Ben Lawrence was hiding something, and most likely either for or with the knowledge of Sarah.

"What's been going on lately?" Tracy climbed up into Nick's lap and Gabe took her legs, absently massaging her calves and feet as they spoke.

"Nothing, really. Our profits are down, but so are everyone's, the economy is crap right now. I've had to break up some fights, deal with inter-Pack stuff, but we haven't beefed with Cascadia. That whole buffer thing was just routine stuff."

"How long have you known you could be Alpha?" Tracy asked, looking straight into his eyes.

He sighed. "Years. But I haven't wanted to be Alpha. I liked my life well enough. I certainly liked my privacy and not having to live at the Pack house. Ben is much older than I am. I was fifteen when he took over Pacific. I could have challenged him even then," he shrugged, "but why? Ben wanted it, he was good with the Pack. And seven years ago he met Sarah and seemed to stabilize even more with a mate. The Pack seemed to like having a mated pair at the helm and I was only twenty-three then anyway."

"You anchored her at twenty-three? No wonder you were so close to her, Nick. Babe, that's a pretty impressionable age to have something so deep happen to you."

Gabe laughed. "Sweetheart, you did say you were twenty-five?"

She tossed her hair back and gave him an imperious look. "I *am* twenty-five. But shit, after a few hours with Sarah, those are like dog years, I think. She's very immature for an Alpha female. And petty. And she needs to wax her chin."

Gabe burst out laughing again and Nick hid a smile beneath his hand. "Remind me to never piss you off."

"And to always deal with unsightly body hair." Nick grinned and kissed her shoulder.

"Okay, first of all, you will piss me off. You are a man and an alpha male, ergo, you will turn into an asshole of epic proportions and I will have to smack you down for it. Deal. And yes, please, I promise to keep the three-inch hairs from my chin if you'll keep your balls nice and smooth for me. They may even get licked that way."

Nick closed his eyes and groaned. "Okay, let's keep focused here or I'm going to lose it. No more talking about licking my anything until we finish here."

"I'm going to ignore that comment about being an asshole and try to not to feel like a creepy old man for having a wife who is sixteen years my junior and instead get back to the topic at hand." Gabe raised an eyebrow at Tracy, who smirked. "Do you think that Ben may have been threatened by your becoming mated? Thinking that perhaps you'd challenge him at last?"

"He and I haven't had any problems lately getting along. We never have. In my entire life the only time I've ever been mad at him has been over stupid shit. Nothing major. The man who shoved you tonight is a stranger to me." And that's what ate at him most.

"Okay, so I know how he acted to my face yesterday but what was his reaction privately?"

"He was...hesitant. I told him briefly on the phone that I'd met my mate but I didn't tell him who. I thought he'd get a kick out of it, you know, some kind of political alliance between Cascadia and Pacific. But when I introduced you that changed. He took me aside and asked me if I was sure you were truly my mate. He seemed agitated. But he was fine to your face. I thought he may have been worried that your Pack was so much stronger and would be in our business a lot."

Tracy laughed. "Well, if Nina wasn't there to restrain Lex and Cade, I don't have any doubt that they'd be up your nose a lot to keep an eye on me—that's how they are. But that's a big brother thing. Cade worries like an old woman and Lex is an insufferable meddler. But Nina keeps them both under her thumb so get that horrified look off your face."

Nick checked his horror. "I don't know, but I want to get to the bottom of this. There's no way I'd have you in a place I felt you were unsafe." Nick pushed a curl back behind her ear.

"Or me. And I don't think it's safe and I think your brother is hiding something a hell of a lot bigger than worry that you'd challenge him. I'm not sure what it is and I don't know him like you do so I could be wrong. But a huge part of my job is based on intuition and I spend all day long reading people. I'd like to talk to him and Sarah more to see what we can see." Gabe looked up at Nick over Tracy's head. "And well, the tri-mate bond thing is going to be tricky enough, my place in the Pack will be problematic."

Nick nodded. "I realize it feels that way and yes, it probably is that way. You rank higher than me so it would be silly of you to give up that to come be Second in Pacific. As our mate, you will be Second as well as you own position in National. I'm sure we can work out an advisory role for you. A mediator on the Enforcer's rank would be really beneficial to us. It'll help me to have another powerful wolf on my side in the inner circle too. Especially in this current situation with Ben and Sarah."

"Okay. I can deal with that." Gabe continued to gently stroke his hands over Tracy's calves.

"Well, and getting back to the current problem—I love you with all my heart, Nick, but I won't be a member of Pacific in this current state. I can join National at Gabe's rank or go back to Cascadia and we can work out the commute. I won't live in that situation and I sure as hell won't hold a pledge to obey Ben or Sarah."

Nick closed his eyes. "I'm sorry for putting you through this. Damn him! I can't lose you, Tracy. I'd go insane if you joined National or went back to Cascadia."

"No matter what happens with that, you won't lose me, Nick. I'm yours, regardless of my Pack affiliation. You could join Cascadia but," she shrugged, "Lex."

"I know. He's *the* Enforcer. Don't think I haven't obsessed over that a bit. God this is fucked up. I won't allow Ben to hold this Pack if he's going insane or going to break it in half. I'll challenge him before I let you be driven away."

"We have a bit before any of that needs to go that way." Gabe tried to stay reasonable.

"And what are you going to do, Gabe? You've said you'd take the Second rank in a ceremonial way. But what do you *want* to do?" Tracy took his hand and kissed his knuckles.

He touched his chin as he thought. "I've been thinking. I'm damned good at what I do. I've trained for the last nearly twenty years to do it. There's no room for me at Pacific. Excuse my bluntness here, but I'm much more powerful than Ben and there is no way I'd be in that Pack without challenging him. Tracy can join National, of course, and we can go bi-coastal. Theoretically, Nick could join National at my rank, but he's not a mediator. I'm not sure where he'd fit in at National. I see some major problems with that."

"Can you take some time off while we deal with this? You're leaving tomorrow?" Panic raced through Tracy at the thought of him leaving.

Sensing her emotions, he pulled her into his lap. "No, honey, I'm not leaving tomorrow. I'll take some time, I have it to take. There are some things brewing that I need to keep an eye on but my assistant will keep me apprised. Do you think I'd just leave you right now? With all this up in the air?"

"I don't know. I'm all over the map here. You have a life in Boston. Friends and family and a Pack. You're important, your job is important so of course I understand that sometimes I'll come second to that. I just," her bottom lip trembled and his heart constricted in his chest, "I don't want you to go away and forget me. I worry that you'll go away and I'll never see you and you'll feel trapped and..." A sob tore through her and he hugged her tight.

He could face the snarling woman, the warrior and the strong-willed mate, but the teary-eyed woman in his lap nearly broke his heart. "Tracy, honey, you don't come second to anything. Not ever. We'll work this out, I promise. But I'm not leaving you. Don't cry, please. I don't want you to cry." He looked up at Nick, who moved to hug her from behind, creating one unified embrace.

"We'll fix this, baby. I swear to you. The three of us will make this work. We're meant to be and so we will be," Nick murmured into her ear. "I love you. Gabe loves you. It's going to be okay." He'd make sure it was.

* * * * *

A thousand miles away, Warren Pellini answered his cell phone. "Hello there, Sarah, and how are you?"

"God damn it! Warren, Nick's mate is Tracy Warden. Tonight at the Pacific Pack house we were wall-to-fucking-wall Cascadia wolves!"

Pellini chuckled. "Well, well, well. Small world, isn't it? I bet that got your tiny heart racing, didn't it?"

"Don't laugh, Warren! This is serious. She's Second now and I don't have the hold on Nick that I had before."

"As long as you stay calm and treat her well, what's the problem? Is it that you can't dangle Nick anymore?"

"She's the problem! She's a pushy bitch. She started all kinds of trouble and they left and Nick and Ben are at each other's throats and Ben is worried that Nick will challenge him and now my meddling in-laws are up in our business. Can't you just have her killed?"

The amused smile slid off Pellini's face and the look that replaced it wasn't friendly at all. "Whyever would you say such a stupid thing, Sarah? That's not funny at all. I would never do such a thing and it's not something to joke about. *Especially on the phone.*" The last was said through clenched teeth in a low growl that raised the hair on Sarah's arms.

"I, uh, I'm sorry. I'm just upset."

"Nevertheless, you need to take care of your own problems, Sarah, and let me remind you that our business is very important to my *family*. If you continue this trouble with the Wardens it does not bode well for our continued relations."

Sarah's heart threatened to burst from her chest. "There's another thing." Her voice was small when she said it but she had no choice. She had to tell him now because if he heard it thirdhand, he'd be even more angry.

"And that is?"

"There's a tri-mate bond."

"Really?" Interest laced his voice. "With who?"

"Nick, Tracy and Gabe Murphy."

"The Mediator? He's there?"

"Yes. There was a border issue to deal with and he came in to mediate it between us and Cascadia. That's how Nick and Tracy met to begin with."

"How much does Nick know about our business relationship?"

"He doesn't. I only told Ben because he figured it out on his own. He's very nervous about it."

Pellini sighed. "Sarah, this is quickly becoming messy. My people hate messy. It takes away from profit and we have to spend entirely too much time cleaning up. I'll think on some things and get back in touch with you." He hung up before she could say anything else.

She put the phone back in the cradle and looked out the window. It was all so damned simple before. She cursed herself again for being stupid enough to seek out Pellini's help when she needed the cash to cover a large transaction she'd floated late the year before. But the deal had been so good, and she'd overextended herself and once the deal was completed she could pay back the accounts she'd drawn on and be square with her clients again.

And the deal had gone very well, but the money was so good and it had been so pleasant dealing with Warren Pellini that she'd gone to him three more times. Until the deal had gone south, leaving her owing a very large sum of money that she should never have taken from her client accounts. Suddenly she'd been facing arrest and jail if anyone found out. She'd had to borrow double from Pellini to pay back the client accounts, leaving her in the hole with the Pellini group. Being the sick bastard he was, he'd taken advantage of that opening and had thrust himself into Pack business and really, before she knew it, Pacific had been laundering large volumes of cash for Pellini.

She never should have gone to Pellini to begin with but she was desperate. The bank wouldn't extend her any more credit and she was on the verge of losing her business. And her greed had gotten her into a world of trouble and with her, the Pack.

Three months before, Ben had found out and confronted her and while he was still really angry with her, he loved her, she was his mate and he wanted to fix it and get the hell out from under the mob.

And now the Pack that hated Pellini and who Pellini hated right back was related to hers and she had a very angry, very nervous mate and had lost her best friend. All because of that bitch Tracy Warden.

Chapter Five

❧

Several boxes of Tracy's clothing and other goods from her house arrived the next morning at the apartment, courtesy of Nina's quick thinking.

Nick raised an eyebrow as she looked for a place to put it all. The problem was that he had as much clothing as she did, which didn't bode well for their present living conditions at all. Hell, he had no idea where Gabe was going to put anything at all.

"Sweetie, can't you leave some of it in a box for now?"

"Nick, you know what? You're an ass. This place is too small." She turned to glare at him. Gabe was on the phone in the study and looked up but kept out of it for the time being.

"I'm an ass because you have too many clothes?"

"*I* have too many clothes? You're a man, Nick, and you have more clothes than I do! You have more pairs of shoes than I do. Oh, okay that's a lie, no one has more shoes than I do, but still, you give me a run for my money. In any case, you're an ass because you want me to keep my clothes in boxes while yours hang up and are in drawers. Way to make me feel at home."

She plopped on the couch.

He sighed, biting back a smile at her comments. "And what would you propose? That I put several thousand-dollar suits in a box while you hang your jeans up?"

Her eyebrow slowly rose and Gabe snorted a laugh and murmured something over the phone.

"I propose that you get some comfortable shoes on. We're meeting the realtor in twenty minutes to go and look at houses. I figure for now we can rent until we figure out just what the hell is going to happen. When we want to buy, did you know that Lex is an architect? He designed the house that he and Nina and Cade live in now. It's been in *Architectural Digest*, you know."

Nick rolled his eyes. "Of course. Can't just be the big bad Enforcer, he has to be some fucking fabulous architect too. Is there anything Lex can't do?"

Tracy laughed. "Well, that took your mind right off me setting up a date to go look at houses to rent. I'll have to keep that in mind for the future." She got up and shoved him in a chair and scrambled atop his lap. "As for what Lex can't do? Why, my darling sweet wolf, he can't be you. And that's everything."

Nick looked up at her, into that face with those big green eyes and those freckles and fell for the thousandth time in the thousandth way. "You're really good, you know that?"

"I have to be to keep you." She rolled her hips, grinding herself over him, and he grabbed her, holding her to him as he arched into her.

She brushed her lips over his and he breathed her in, letting her presence calm and soothe him.

"Let's go in the bedroom," he murmured, kissing her chin.

"Can't. We have to leave soon to meet the realtor at her office." Her hands in his hair, she pulled him up so that their lips were touching again. "But I definitely want a rain check."

"Can't you call her? Put it back a few hours?"

"Nope." She stood up and straightened her clothes. "It is my plan to have a place by the end of today if it kills you and Gabe. I want my dog here, I want my own closet. I want a place that doesn't have echoes of your past conquests."

He winced and Gabe walked up behind her and encircled her waist with his arms. "Hi, sweetness. You giving Nick a hard time?"

"I am not!" she said with mock indignation. "It's time to get ready to go see the realtor. So let's go."

Once they all got downstairs to the garage, they piled into Gabe's rental because Nick's Porsche was too small for the three of them.

"And where am I going?" Nick asked Tracy with a smile.

"I looked through your Pack address book and called Shelley. The other realtor you wanted to use was part of that whole mess last night and I don't want any part of that. But she didn't seem to be and I saw that she worked for a realty company and when I called and chatted with her she had a lot of great ideas. I'm sure you know where she works."

Nick sat there looking at her. "You called Shelley? You know that she and I...that we..."

"Oh stop stuttering." Tracy waved her hand. "It's fine. I know what she was to you and I know what I am to you. Even better, she knows it too. So let's get moving. I want to find a place to live and I want to do it today."

Gabe knew better than to even suggest that it might take some time to find a place. She'd proven to him that she could pretty much move mountains by sheer will and so he just sat back and handled some Pack business on his cell phone on the way to the realtor's.

Once there, each male took one of her arms and they garnered a few curious looks as they went into the office. Shelley stood near the reception desk speaking with someone when she saw them come in.

"Hi!" She approached with a smile, and ignoring Gabe and Nick, kissed Tracy's cheek. "You look great. Let's go back to my office and I'll show you a few places I think would be good for you all." Looking up briefly at Nick and Gabe, she motioned her head toward her doorway and they followed.

Once inside, Tracy sat next to Shelley and they discussed the listings on rentals in the area, the various amenities and drawbacks to each one. In the end, they found four to go look at and rejected a few.

Tracy rode with Shelley in her car while the men, Nick finally giving up the argument, followed in their car.

"It drives him crazy to imagine what I might be telling you," Shelley said with a laugh as they drove.

Tracy laughed. "Oh I know anyway. Why wouldn't he have slept with you? You're gorgeous and he's hot. It seems a natural thing. But you certainly seem to be fine with it so what's the problem?"

The redhead looked at her from the corner of her eye. "Well, yes. I'm just amazed you think so. I mean, after what went down last night I'm surprised you're even speaking to any of us. I can't believe it all happened the way it did. God, you must think we're all a bunch of savages."

"I think that there's something going on that I don't understand but I don't blame all of Pacific for it. Do you have any ideas?" Tracy asked casually, wondering what Shelley would say, if anything at all.

"Well, if you're asking me, I'd have to say I think Sarah is behind it. She and Jo are bosom buddies, you know, and Jo is dumb as a rock. Way too stupid to have thought that little scene up on her own. And that stuff on the porch? Well, I don't know the whole story but it sounded like Sarah was in the wrong somehow and you took her to task for it. And good for you."

Tracy briefly outlined the situation with the phone call and Shelley was scandalized. "You have to be kidding me! I'd have killed the bitch!"

Tracy laughed. "I seriously wanted to for a while but Nick wanted so much for things to be all right that I let it go. I mean, I knew part of her apology was for Nick's benefit but I didn't know *all* of it was! I just have a hard time believing last night was about her wanting Nick to herself. I mean, she's risking tearing the Pack apart with this. She has to know that Nick is my mate. She doesn't stand a chance."

Shelley shook her head as they pulled into the driveway of the first house. "I don't know, Tracy. It all seems very suspicious to me. But there've been some..." She stopped speaking as Nick came to the door to open it for Tracy.

"Tell me later if you don't feel comfortable saying it in front of Nick," she murmured and let him open her door.

By the third house, Shelley had told Tracy that she'd gone out with the wolf who'd handled the basic accounting for the Pack and he'd quit and gone tight-lipped. In the end, he'd actually left the Pack. Shelley had thought it odd at the time but figured he'd felt like there was no real room for him in the Pack hierarchy and that's why he'd left. She hadn't thought of it again until she'd started thinking about how odd Ben and Sarah had been acting and when it'd all started up.

"Is it okay if I talk to Nick about this? I think he should know. I promise you he won't be upset with you."

"Okay. I don't know much more than that. Like I said, I'd forgotten it entirely until last night."

When they pulled up the long driveway leading to the last house, Tracy sat stunned. They drove up a hill and when they reached the top, there sat a Spanish Colonial, complete with a courtyard, fountain and gardens.

"Oh my goodness, who'd have expected this?" There was a lovely circular drive and lots of room at the sides of the house. It was not very common to see that style of architecture in the Northwest and Tracy instantly fell in love with the circular arches and the pretty gardens.

She was out the door before Gabe or Nick could get there, staring, openmouthed, at the house.

"This place just opened up yesterday. The same family that had it built ten years ago has moved to London. They're good friends of mine but they don't know if it'll be for a year or permanent just yet. They are very nice people. The rent isn't too high for a place this big." The details Shelley was giving floated around Tracy as they walked into the open front hallway. The tile was a warm red glaze with pretty blue, cream and yellow accents inset here and there. The ceilings were high and big windows lined the first floor, flooding the house with light.

There were five bedrooms and huge closets. The kitchen was a dream with a huge island and a giant fridge and freezer. A cook's fantasy. It looked out over a very large fenced yard with a pretty view. No immediate neighbors to either side.

"I'd ask what you think but, baby, you have no poker face at all." Nick grinned at her. "What do you think, Gabe?"

"It's beautiful and clearly Tracy loves it. When can we move in?"

"I just need to run a credit report and get a deposit and the first and last month's rent and you can have the keys."

"Milton is going to love the yard. Dogs are okay, right?"

"I'm sure if it was a stranger, no. But I know Nick and I know he'll take care of the house and I can vouch for you with them."

"Let's do it. Can you handle selling my apartment?" Nick put his arm around Tracy, unable to not touch her.

"Hell yes! I'll buy the damned thing, I've wanted that place for two years now. No offense, Tracy, but I think most of his appeal, other than the face, was that apartment."

Caught by surprise, Tracy laughed. "Well, you can have the apartment, I'll keep the face."

Shelley grabbed her hand and squeezed. "You've got a deal."

They all drove back to the office, filled out paperwork, wrote a check and got the keys. Tracy hugged Shelley on the way out. "Thanks for everything. And thanks for telling me all of that stuff. I appreciate it. I don't know anyone down here and it's nice feeling like I may have a friend."

Shelley smiled. "You do have a friend. Truly. I'd love to grab a drink or lunch with you soon, get to know you better. Call me if you need anything else and I'll keep my eyes and ears open."

"Thanks."

Grinning, she rode back to the apartment with Gabe and Nick.

"Okay, I admit it, the house is gorgeous. Good choice, baby." Nick grinned at her, taking her hand and kissing her palm until shivers ran from the heat of his mouth straight to her pussy.

"Well, my. Yes. I'm glad you like it. And it's got space for all of us and a yard for Milton. He will love that fountain and oh, the indoor pool and weight room will come in handy, won't they?"

Gabe laughed. "I like seeing you this way. In fact, I think I'm going to do my level best to keep you like this all the time." He leaned forward and kissed her shoulder.

"Well, I am happy. And I need to deal with my house. My grandmother is still alive but she won't want it. I tried to get her to let me buy it when my grandfather died and left it to me but she refused. She lives in a swank condo community for hot seniors near my parents. I could sell it, but it's been in my family since it was built."

"What about one of your sisters? Another member of your family? Do you think one of them would want it?" Nick thought about her family he'd met at the joining.

"Well, my cousin Dave and Megan live at the house with Cade, Nina and Lex. Tegan may want it, she has loved it and she's in an apartment right now. I'll have to ask her. Of course, she'll insist on paying for the damned thing because that's how she is. She won't take anything from anyone."

"Tegan is Megan's twin?"

"Yes but they couldn't be more different. Megan is outgoing and funny but Tegan is so serious. She's a lot like

Cade. She's a good person and someone you can always count on but she hates to count on anyone else. She had a mate, you know. They met and married when she was twenty and he was nineteen. Oh man, were they ever in love! But he was killed in Afghanistan several years ago. And her anchor was already mated to someone so it wasn't as if she could have pursued anything with him anyway. She's been so aloof ever since." One had the option of pursuing a relationship with her anchor, as a bond had been established on some level. But if the anchor was mated, the female would be alone.

Nick's stomach clenched at the thought of losing her. The emptiness one must feel after the death of a mate! It terrified him. He met Gabe's eyes in the rearview mirror and knew Gabe had been thinking the same thing. An unspoken bond formed between them to keep her safe at all costs.

"I'm sorry, baby. I can't imagine how painful that must have been for her."

"Yeah, she doesn't talk about it much. She and Layla, my other sister, are closest, and even Lay has felt shut out sometimes. Anyway, I should go up there and deal with all of this myself. Deal with the store, the house, bring back my car and my furniture and Milty."

"Not by yourself you won't," Gabe growled from the backseat. "Nick, myself or both of us will accompany you. We don't know what is going on with Sarah and Ben and until we do, I plan to keep an extra close watch on you."

That chafed but she understood it. "Don't you have to go to Boston too?"

"Boston can wait a few days. There's trouble brewing, but if this isn't resolved when I need to get back you'll come with me. I don't want you here with all of this insanity."

They pulled into the parking garage and went into the elevator, where both men pressed against her until she could barely think. "When you do that, I can't think straight," she sighed as Nick slid his lips down her neck.

"Good." His hands moved up her torso as Gabe ground himself into her ass, his hands moving inside her sweater and cupping her breasts.

The elevator came to a stop and they all groaned and spilled out into the hall, adjusting clothing and rushing to the apartment.

Being pushed back to the carpet with Nick over her, she put her hand out to stop him and turned his head by his chin, showing him the phone. "Thirty-two messages. You'd better see what it is. Could be an emergency, god knows it's been that kind of week."

He sighed and sat up with a growl. Gabe helped her up and pushed her against the wall. "While he's busy, I'll just keep you occupied."

But they were both listening to the calls and stopped to go over to the couch, where Nick was watching the machine wearily.

There were several messages from his father, a few from Ben, more from Sarah and various others from different members of the Pack, both for and against him. Tracy put her hand against his cheek.

"My father wants to work things out within the family and show a united front to the rest of the Pack. Josh wants me to challenge Ben. Ben wants to try and work it out, Sarah wants me to apologize to Ben. And a whole lot of 'what are you thinking' and 'kick his ass and protect your mate'. I don't know what to think."

"I forgot to tell you a few things Shelley told me. She seemed to think there may be some suspicious reason behind the wolf who was your accountant's leaving the Pack. Have there been any financial irregularities that you know of?"

"Well, there should have been a fairly large bit of cash moving through after the lumber sales. First we did the sale of the raw lumber and then we sold the land and the mill. The mill was worked by our wolves and wasn't profitable and hadn't been for years. Most of the families have moved here to Portland or out to the coast where we have a resort the Pack owns. And then we moved the capital into other projects and some into basic stuff like the health insurance for the Pack and the pension program. Our accountant did get a bit squirrelly at the end but I just chalked it up to not having a lot of single women. He told me he was leaving for a Pack with more females in it."

"I don't know. But I think you should look into it."

"You can't seriously think that my brother is stealing from his own Pack?" Nick pushed up off the couch and began to pace.

"I said I didn't know and I don't. I didn't say anything about Ben anyway. But it seems a big coincidence and coincidences are suspicious. Have you had money problems and then it got better, a lot better, with the sale?" Tracy was stung but tried to remember how hard it must be for him.

"And lay off her, Nick. It's not her fault for telling you the truth and it sure as hell isn't her fault that your brother and his mate are up to something." Gabe wasn't so understanding, Tracy was his to protect too.

"You think I like this? Being hurt that my mate is accusing my brother of something?"

"You think I like coming into your family and being attacked and maligned? Having the female you're anchored to say all of that stuff to try and put a wedge between us? You think I wanted my mate's Pack to hate me for some unknown reason? You think I want this to be happening to you and hurting you, Nick? Is that what you think?"

He turned and sank to his knees, putting his head on her lap. "I'm sorry. I know you aren't trying to hurt me. I'm sorry my family is acting this way. I don't understand it."

She bent her head over his and massaged his scalp. "I know. I'm sorry it's happening to you and I just want to get to the bottom of it. If Ben is in trouble, you should know why so you can help him."

"I hate the idea of having to go over there again and bring you into the middle of that. You should stay back here until I figure it all out."

"Yeah, sure. I'll just wait here for you and paint my toenails. Oh no, wait, I'm Second in the Pack and your mate, guess I'll do my job and be there. Dumbass, you actually think I'd stay here while you did this all yourself?"

He started to speak but saw the hard set of her mouth and sighed deeply. It was time to put away his feelings as a brother and be the Enforcer of his clan. If he had to challenge his brother to save Pacific and Tracy, he would. Period.

"Too bad the Mediator is so utterly biased in this case." Tracy sent Gabe a weak smile and he returned it, leaning in quickly to kiss the tip of her nose.

"You have to see this through. Not just to figure out what's wrong to protect Tracy, but to protect the Pack. It's your duty. I'll help in whatever way I can." Gabe looked at Nick, who'd sat back on the couch.

"Yes, it's my duty. And I'll do it because I'm the Enforcer and it's my job to protect my Pack." Nick took a deep breath and Tracy watched in awe as he pulled on his rank like a suit of armor. Sitting there, he radiated strength and power and menace.

"Wow, I know I'm not supposed to say this, but you're really hot when you're all badass."

The look he sent her made heat spread outward from low in her gut. When he spoke, his voice was low and the bass in it vibrated down her spine. "I'm going to take you when this is over and my wolf is riding me, Tracy. I'm going to bury myself deep in your cunt and Gabe is going to fill you from behind. I'm going to mark you here," he touched her neck where it met her shoulder, "and anywhere else that appeals to me."

She blinked several times, feeling slightly lightheaded.

Gabe leaned in to growl in her ear. "Maybe I'll put a chain through these rings," his hands moved to her breasts, "and bind your hands. I'd like that, to see you bound and at my pleasure. At our pleasure. Perhaps even bring out the blindfold so you won't know what you'll feel next."

She closed her eyes and let the image of that float through her system, making her feel heavy and warm.

Nick chuckled. "I think she likes that, Gabe."

"Good, because I think we need a very large four-poster bed so that we can make use of the many ways to spread and bind her. Do you like rope, sweetheart?"

She shook herself out of her fantasy to answer. "Rope?"

"Mmm-hmmm. I think we've got a lot of things to try together, don't you, Nick?"

"Most definitely." Nick's face was very close to Tracy's and also to Gabe's. Their mingled scent drove Tracy insane with need.

"Please fuck me," she whispered as Nick's hands worked at the button and zipper of her jeans.

Gabe pulled her sweater over her head and was back, hands on her breasts, mouth brushing hot kisses against the back of her neck.

"Stand up," Nick said and she obeyed, both men still sitting. Nick pushed her jeans and panties down her legs and she stepped out of them and was there totally naked as both of them raked their eyes over her, devouring every detail of her body.

"You're so beautiful there in the late afternoon sun, Tracy. Your skin nearly glows with the light. I love the way your back curves. You have such long legs but tiny feet. I don't think I've seen a wolf with such petite features before." Gabe stood and she heard his belt jingle as he loosened his pants and the hiss of the material as they hit the floor.

"Petite? I'm five-ten. That's not petite." Her voice nearly broke at the heat of him as he moved close behind her. She watched Nick pull off his shirt, exposing his chest and the flat, hard muscle there.

"Yes you're tall, but you have a pixie nose and freckles across your cheeks and a sweet mouth to go with those tiny feet. It's your features that are petite." Gabe spoke as he took her wrists and she felt the cool leather of his belt wrap around them. "Is this all right with you?" He spoke softly as he tightened the belt, binding her hands and lower arms.

Excitement coursed through her body. "Yes. I trust you."

Nick stood, removing his pants and boxers, tossing them into the chair behind him. He was so hard that her mouth watered and her clit pulsed.

"Good. Now, let's move to the chaise." Gabe tugged on her wrists gently.

"With the windows open like that? Anyone could see in!"

"Why, yes, yes they could. Does that excite you, Tracy? Knowing that someone sitting at their desk doing work could look up and see us through the windows? See you fucking two men? See your naked body writhing? See you with my cock in your mouth?" Gabe half sat, half lay on the chaise, widening his thighs so she'd be able to kneel there.

"I..." The idea of someone perhaps catching them did turn her on. Oh gracious she was bad! There she stood, totally naked, hands and arms tied with a belt, getting ready to have sex with two men. She grinned. Yep, despite everything else, life was fucking good.

"That's right, baby. You can't deny that it turns you on. I can smell how much it turns you on, I can hear it as you walk. Your nipples are rock-hard and you keep licking your lips." Nick spoke as he helped position her because her wrists were still bound. He knelt behind her as she leaned down to Gabe. He held his cock so that she could take it into her mouth.

"Nice and slow and keep me wet. You're so good, Tracy. Your mouth is sooo good," Gabe crooned and ran fingertips over her shoulders and the back of her neck.

She moaned and arched her back when Nick held her open with one hand and thrust into her snug heat in one thrust.

"Oh god yes," Nick murmured, catching her wrists in one hand to help her stay up as she moved her mouth over Gabe's cock. What a sight she made there between them! So sexy and outright hot it melted his control. He wasn't sure he'd ever been so turned on in his life. But each time he was with this woman, he thought that. Each time he touched her, he needed her more than the last time he did.

The way her body felt wrapped around his cock was so good that he wasn't sure his system could process it all. He'd always loved sex, had it quite often with many beautiful women and not one experience he'd ever had before he met Tracy could even compare. With her—inside her, touching her, smelling her, feeling her body against his—he was whole. He belonged to her, to them.

Nick watched her love Gabe with her mouth, watched Gabe's hand gently caress her neck and shoulders. Tenderness burst through him for them both. He felt an intense connection to these two wolves he found himself bound to. If he hadn't, Nick wasn't sure they could have made the threesome work. But he felt as emotionally bonded to Gabe as he did to Tracy. A deep sense of kinship ran between them, held them all together as a unit.

Tracy drowned in the intensity of her need for them. Her hands bound, it was Nick who held her up. Her eyes closed against the sight of Gabe, so beautiful in his sexuality that she couldn't bear it. It was Gabe's hand at her neck and shoulders that gentled her.

Into her pussy Nick would thrust, and down her mouth descended over Gabe's cock. Nick's gasp when she tightened around him was echoed by Gabe's moan as she took him as far back into her throat as she could.

Each man filled her to the point of nearly overflowing and that fullness was soul deep. She was a strong woman, and yet submitting to them in the way she was felt so right too. Giving herself over to them both took trust, yes, but she had no hesitation in doing it.

Gabe watched her through half-lidded eyes. Watched her mouth take his cock deep over and over. Was entranced by the way her lashes fell against her cheeks. Loved the way her breasts moved each time Nick thrust into her pussy, causing the little bead in each nipple ring to swing forward.

She was gloriously beautiful to him. He loved her scent and the soft sounds of pleasure she made around his cock. So much had clicked into place that despite the utter chaos of the Pacific Pack and whatever the hell Ben and Sarah Lawrence were hiding, he'd never felt more right.

The heat and wet of her mouth sent him hurtling toward orgasm, and by the look on Nick's face he wasn't far behind.

"Make her come, Nick," Gabe murmured. Nick's mouth curved at one corner and he slid his hand from her hip to her lips.

"Wet my fingers, baby." He reached down to where her mouth was. His fingers slid against Gabe's cock and electricity shot up his arm. His gaze locked with Gabe's for a moment before Tracy pulled off his cock and sucked Nick's fingers into her mouth, wetting them before he took them to her pussy, stroking over her clit.

He sucked in a breath as her pussy fluttered and tightened around him. "Mmmm. That's it, baby. Come for me."

Gabe moved his hand from her neck to roll one of her delicious little nipples between his fingers, pulling the ring in the way he knew she liked. He sure as hell knew she liked it at that moment because she made a soft sound of pleasure around his cock and lost her rhythm for a few moments.

Her clit was hard and swollen beneath Nick's fingertips and her thighs began to tremble as she pressed back against him harder to take him deeper. "Oh that's good. Give it to me."

"Fuck," Gabe hissed as he began to come, body tightening as he pinched her nipple tighter, feeling as if his whole body was shooting out the head of his cock into her. "Oh I do love you."

Tracy made a surprised sound as her orgasm hit her full force. Waves of intense pleasure buffeted her, threatening to pull her under. Her hands were bound and there was an element of letting go there as she let Nick do the work of holding her up and gave over to the feelings rushing through her body and her heart.

She felt the muscles in Nick's thighs and abdomen tighten and he hoarsely whispered her name as he came deep within her body.

Muscles still twitched and small aftershocks of pleasure still racked her body as she dimly felt Nick remove the belt. Gabe rubbed her wrists and they lay her down on the carpet, each man settling in beside her.

* * * * *

After a few minutes more she finally opened her eyes and saw Nick above her, smiling down. She reached up to touch his cheek and run her fingertips through his hair. "Wow."

Gabe laughed beside her and kissed her shoulder. "Yeah, wow is an understatement, I think."

"No offense to you both or anything. You are both extraordinarily handsome and strong and the utter hotness and all, but I think this mate thing is like a sex amplifier." Her words were still slightly slurred. Each time they were together as a threesome she drowned in the pleasure until she was drunk on endorphins. It was still amazing when it was one-on-one, but as a triad the energy they put out together was tremendous.

"Is that a complaint?" Nick's smile was arrogant and she couldn't help but blush.

"Hell no. I wish I could bottle it up. We'd make a billion dollars."

A cell phone rang in the distance.

"That's me." Gabe groaned as he rolled up onto his knees and got up to go to his pants and dig out his phone.

Tracy half listened to the conversation as she turned back to Nick. "So when are we going to get over to the Pack house?"

"I'll call my father to set it up. I'm going to call Josh and get him and a few others who are loyal to me there just in case."

"Are you going to challenge Ben?" She sat up and grabbed her shirt, pulling it back on.

"If I have to, yes."

"Okay. I'm going to call Nina to get her help on something."

He frowned when she put her shirt back on and sighed when she handed his over. "Nina's help on what?" He put the shirt back on and she stood, holding out her hand, and he grabbed it to stand with her.

She walked down the hall and into the bathroom and he followed her, leaning against the door, watching her clean up and pull panties and socks back on, followed by a pair of jeans.

"Damn, those are fine jeans. I think you should wear something baggy. I saw the way Josh was looking at you last night. I can't kill him, I need him at my back right now."

She looked shocked for a moment and then rolled her eyes. Kissing him on her way back out, she put extra sway in her step just for his amusement.

"This is just between us, but Nina was the shit back in the day. She's a superstar computer hacker. That's how we found out all that shit about the embezzlement of our Third and the involvement of that twisted fuck, Warren Pellini."

"Pellini?" Gabe walked back into the room, having changed his clothes and finished his phone call. "Why are you talking about him?"

"Last year our Third was embezzling money from the Pack to pay back a huge debt to the Pellini Family. He stole some of the lycanthropy virus and sold it to the rogues. Then he killed Nina's brother and nearly killed her too, in a challenge at the Pack house."

"I remember hearing about that. But she got a gun and nearly killed him, right?" Nick remembered hearing about it and having a swell of admiration for Nina Warden.

Tracy nodded. "But not before the sick bastard bit her. There's still a lot of major resentment from Nina on this whole thing."

"That Carter tried to kill her? Or changed her illegally? He was stripped of rank, right?" Nick watched her put her boots on and noted she chose the Doc Martens with the thick sole. He smiled, knowing she'd chosen them in case she had to throw down.

"That, but also that she was a human and nearly killed while the Pack stood there and didn't help. That Lex and Cade didn't help. Although Lex did have to be disarmed and held down by several other wolves while he screamed that he was going to rip Carter to shreds when he got free. It's been a big issue between them."

"She's right. I think the whole notion is messed up. Cade should have stopped it." Gabe leaned against the counter. Tracy's eye was drawn to him. Long and tall and broad-shouldered. Substantial. The sun streaming into the hallway glinted off the reddish highlights in his caramel hair and she could see the strands of gray here and there as well as his salt-and-pepper at the temples. She loved the lines around his eyes, those deep brown, very serious eyes. He was dignified and elegant and sensual. A shiver rode her for a moment as she caught his scent.

"Cade has a responsibility to his Pack to maintain order. She was a human and therefore had no rank in the Pack. His Third had every right to challenge, even if it was cowardly. If Cade had stopped it, how could the Pack ever depend on him to make hard choices for the good of the whole Pack in the future? He can't choose his anchored bond over the Pack." Nick couldn't imagine watching Tracy be challenged like that. Thank god she was a wolf and had his protection and rank.

"Oh bullshit. Being a wolf in this century means we can let go of some of the old ways that used to be so life and death. We can afford to change. We have to. I understand the other wolves standing aside. Cade is clearly an Alpha that holds his Pack, it would have been impossible to disobey his orders. But Cade didn't have to make that choice. Cade was free to stop it. In not doing so, he held to the old ways, which strangle us and keep us from moving forward."

Tracy understood Gabe's point more than she would have before she became so close to Nina. But Nick was old school. He'd been born a wolf and into a ruling family. Of course he'd see a need to uphold tradition, it's how he would have been raised and educated. But Gabe hadn't started out a wolf, he had a human sensibility, and she agreed with him that it was important for Packs to democratize.

"Okay, anyway," Tracy interrupted the argument, "I think it's an interesting discussion and I have my own feelings on the issue but right now let's get back to the topic. Nina the super hacker. I'm going to ask her to snoop around in the Pack accounts to see what she can turn up."

"Nina's a hacker?" Gabe grinned. "She's a woman of many talents, I see."

"If you say anything else about her with that look on your face I'll scratch your eyes out," Tracy growled and both men started at the change in her mood.

"Oh you can't do that unless you're going to be bending over the arm of the couch so I can fuck the sense back into you." Gabe moved toward her, his wolf aroused at her display of dominance.

"I can do whatever I want if you think you're going to talk about another female like that in my presence." Eyes narrowed, she moved to him and his mouth was on hers, hand in her hair, holding her to him so that he could devour her.

He broke the kiss and looked down into her face. Her head was back, neck exposed to him fully, eyes still sparking at him. "Woman, what you do to me," he murmured and skated his lips over her jawline and down her throat. "You wreck me as much as you complete me." Moving back up to look into her face again, he caught the curve of her lips in a smile of utter female satisfaction.

"It does cheer me, yes, to know I have that effect on you."

"We've created a monster," Nick said in the background.

"Mmm-hmm. You'd best keep me satisfied then, hadn't you?" Tracy winked at Nick and stepped out of Gabe's embrace. "Now, I'm calling Nina. Do you have any basic info like a checkbook or account number where she can start?"

Nick swallowed hard as he followed her into the office. That bit of dominance play she'd engaged in out there with Gabe had fried his circuits. Pulling out a file from a drawer, he placed it on the desk in front of her. "This is all I've got. I'm going in the other room to call my father." He leaned in and brushed his lips over her forehead and left, closing the door.

Gabe nipped in a moment later. "I'm just going to watch you work. I have some suspicions about Pellini that I'd like to discuss with you later."

She nodded and picked up the phone to call Nina.

After explaining the situation, Nina got down to business and asked a million questions and promised to look into it and call her back when she found out anything.

Nick came in to tell them that a meeting had been arranged for the following day at the Pack house and Tracy told him Nina was looking into the account information.

"Whatever will we do for the next twenty-four hours?" Nick's eyebrow rose.

"Go to Seattle so I can get my house in order and get my dog. Get some furniture for the new house. I'm calling Cade right back to arrange to come up. We'll stay at my house tonight." Tracy grinned and neither man had the heart to stop her, she looked so damned happy.

Chapter Six
฿

They drove straight to Tracy's. Nick was impressed by the explosion of color when he walked into the living room. Orange and red and blue and yellow, it should have been too much but she'd made it work. He made a mental note to let her have free rein in decorating the house.

He frowned though, as he caught sight of the dozens of pictures all over the place with her and various people, various *male* people. "Who are these people?" he called back over his shoulder.

"Friends and family." She amazed him. She was one of the most efficient people he'd ever met. She'd already called a moving company on the way up and they were due to have dinner with her family at Cade's shortly. She was looking through her stuff and distracted but still doing three things at once.

"*Friends?*"

She looked up and saw his look and snorted a laugh. "Yes, some of them are friends. Others are…were *friends*. Don't worry," she held back a smile, "I won't hang them up at the house."

"You'd better not or your eyes might get scratched out," Gabe called out from the couch, where he'd been on the phone.

"Ha! I'll drive over to Cade's in my car. We'll bring Milton back here tonight and he'll ride down with me tomorrow morning."

Nick stifled a sigh and just nodded. "One of us will ride with you too."

"Why?"

"Safety." He said it like she was simple, and she understood Nina's frustration with Cade a lot better.

"You gonna protect me from poor gas mileage?"

Gabe watched, amused. Nick was a dumbass, handling her the way he did. Gabe had the wisdom that came with age and knew that a frontal attack was the wrong way to deal with her. Of course he wanted to protect her as well, but he knew it would happen a lot easier if it was a spur-of-the-moment thing instead of a patronizing command. *Oh pup, watch and learn.* He smiled in Nick's direction, knowing he'd swoop in tomorrow, butter her up and ride back, having her all to himself.

"Enough, children. Let's go to dinner, shall we? And then we're going to talk about Pellini and what I've learned today." Gabe stood up and they all headed out.

* * * * *

Nick tried to ignore what an insane driver Tracy was, but it was nearly impossible with his life flashing before his eyes every three minutes. Since Gabe had been in the backseat on the way up, he rode in the backseat now and was glad to not have to watch out the front windshield as she careened all over the place.

"Holy shit, woman. You should think about driving NASCAR or something," he mumbled and Gabe heard him, barking out a laugh.

"Shaddup, Porsche boy. Anyway, we're almost there so you can stop digging your fingers into the seats. Jeez, I'm gonna have to charge you for the damage."

She pulled up a long drive and approached big iron gates.

"Some setup." Gabe was clearly impressed with the situation.

"Not bad at all, huh?" She rolled down the window, keyed in a code and the gates swung open to admit the car.

Around the curve in the drive the house came into view and both men gave low whistles.

"Wow. Yeah, of course he's a fucking amazing architect too. Can't just be the best Enforcer. Oh no, he's got to be superwolf. It's enough to give a man a complex."

She pulled into one of the garage bays and turned off the car. Turning around, she crawled into the backseat and onto his lap. "Hey, you, hot Enforcer guy with the totally hot mate. Lex has nothing on you, so stop it. I love you." She leaned in and brushed her lips over his and closed her eyes as the warmth of contact spread through her.

Gabe growled. "Honey, this is not the time. You start it and I'm gonna want to finish it. Right here in the garage of your brothers' house." He turned in the seat, watching them both.

Nick laughed at the idea of getting caught in a threesome by her family.

Tracy sighed. "Okay, you're right. But did you know that the counters at my house are about your waist height?" She said this as she got out of the car and both men groaned before following her.

Milton came bounding in as the three of them entered the house. Barking excitedly, he gave Tracy a goofy grin and head-butted her until she knelt and hugged him, kissing his head.

"Milton, my darling boy! Mommy has missed you. But guess what? We got a house just for you and you're coming home with me tonight." She continued to babble to the dog while both men looked on and finally up to see Lex shaking his head.

"Nick, Gabe, welcome. You two want a drink? The whole family is in there, I'd suggest a double." Lex shook their hands and leaned down to kiss Tracy's head. "Hey, pumpkin. How are you?"

She stood and he hugged her tight. She knew that he had to wrestle down his impulse to order Nick and Gabe out of there and make her stay so he could protect her. It touched her deeply but they both knew it wasn't his job anymore. He stepped back and tipped her chin up to look into her face closely.

"I'm good. Despite all of this other stuff, Lex, despite it all I've found the other parts of me. They're good, that's good. It's all this other shit that sucks."

He nodded and looked over at Nick and Gabe with a slight narrowing of his eyes. "Come on in then, let's get everyone a drink."

Nina held back and hugged Tracy. "I've found some stuff, sweetie. I don't know if Nick is going to be happy about it."

"Oh god, that bad?" Alarm raced through her.

"I don't know. It's dodgy, no doubt about it. But let's talk it out. Gabe told Cade that there was some stuff about Pellini he wanted to discuss. I think we need to lay it all out on the table and see what we've got."

Suddenly Gabe was standing there, having sensed her distress. "Honey? Is everything all right?"

"I don't know, Gabe. Let's go in and eat and then we'll see."

* * * * *

Dinner was a fairly raucous event. The very long table was lined with every Warden sibling and his or her mate, if there was one. Tracy's parents and grandmother were there as well as her niece and nephew and three cousins who were part of Cade's security detail.

The din was pretty deafening at times, and it amused Tracy to watch them all in action and Nick's and Gabe's response to it all. Nick seemed to be at home around such a loud table but there was sadness around his eyes. She hoped very much that they could figure all of this out to save his family. Gabe seemed entertained and slightly overwhelmed. She realized that she didn't know much about him and resolved to draw out his story. It brought home just how new their relationship was. The beauty of the mate bond was deep love and connection but she didn't know either one of her men very well.

The men decided to clean up after the meal and the women all headed into the living room to wait for them to discuss the whole issue of Pacific and Pellini.

Tracy took Tegan aside and asked her about the house, and as she'd predicted, Tegan was interested but insisted that she pay for it.

"Why? He was your grandfather too. He only left it to me because you all had places to live."

Tegan rolled her eyes at her little sister. "He left it to you because you loved it and because you took such good care of him and of that house. And you've spent a lot of time and money on it since you moved in. He left me his '56 Caddy and the rest of us got things that meant a lot to us. You have a new life starting up and you'll need the money."

In a family of blonds, Tegan and Layla were the only ones who'd inherited their maternal grandmother's fiery red. Her green eyes and the jut of her chin were pretty much the same stubborn set that the other Wardens had though, and Tracy sighed seeing it.

In the end, they decided to have Tegan rent to own the house and pay more as she could. Both of them felt like they'd won something in the argument and the house stayed in the family.

When all of the males came back into the room the amount of testosterone hit the roof, and all the mated females wore secret smiles and squirmed a bit.

Gabe settled in on one side of Tracy and Nick on the other. She felt utterly safe snuggled between them and Milton lay at her feet. A girl could get used to all this male adulation. She shot a grin at Nina, who snorted a laugh.

"I'd ask what that was about but I really don't want to know," Cade muttered dryly. "So we've established that Tracy, Nick and Gabe have a tri-mate bond and we've allowed Grandma to crow about it and I'm sure that Mom is so pleased she'll give those of us who are yet to be mated a break for a little while." He shot a hopeful look at his mother, who waved him off.

"Anyway, Gabe has some things to tell us about the Pellini Group before Nina tells us what she found out about the Pacific Pack bank records that she illegally hacked into earlier this afternoon." With that, Cade shot a glare at Tracy, who gave him a discreetly raised middle finger as she scratched her nose.

Gabe sat forward instead of standing up. This was his family now and he didn't want to push his rank. "As you're aware, the Pellini family has found the ear of the Second in the National Pack. I've been more and more concerned by this in the last six months as I've seen the Pellini people have more of a say in Pack business. This makes me very unhappy and I've been concerned as I watched them get their claws into the National Pack. But I'm Third," he shrugged, "and what the Second does is something I need to be careful over. And it's something that Pellini has used in his whisperings to the Second. He's made me look like a traitor and someone out to usurp the Second's position. So each time someone comes to me worried about the situation, I have to reassure them."

"But you don't feel very reassured?" Cade asked.

"No. No I don't, and my being away right now only exacerbates things because I'm a voice of reason in the inner circle. When I'm not around, it makes it easier for the Second to get to the Alpha."

"Well, we've had our share of worries. As you probably know, we've had our own problems with the Pellini family in the last few years. We can never seem to get enough on them. Even after we had the run-in with them that got Carter executed and dumped on our land, we couldn't prove that they were the ones behind the stolen virus or the hit. And we don't know if they reproduced any of the virus to use later. So you can understand our concern that suddenly a murderer and criminal like Warren Pellini has the ear of one of the most powerful wolves in the country." Lex took a drink of his beer.

"I can't go into all of it, but there have been some less-than-ideal business decisions made because of Pellini's involvement. People who've confronted him on it have been fired or challenged or threatened. I've been threatened but my position is more solid than a lot of others because the Alpha trusts me greatly. But he also trusts the Second.

"So what I'd like to do is find out where the Packs are on this. I've spoken with Great Lakes, Shasta, City of Angels and Golden Gate and they're all with me. I hate to put you on the spot but this is a serious situation and will only get worse until we get Pellini out of there."

Lex took a quick look at Cade, who gave a small nod. "We're with you. What do you need?"

"Right now, nothing. I'm hoping this will be bloodless and reasonable. If I can go to the Alpha and show him that the Packs of the nation are concerned about Pellini and want him out, I believe he'll make that happen."

"Okay. We've got your back."

He turned to Nick. "And Pacific?"

Nick shrugged. "I can't speak for the Pack, obviously. But if you're asking what the Enforcer thinks, I think the Pellini Family is bad news and they endanger all of us. If the humans had any idea there was such a thing as werewolf organized crime it could lead to some very frightening times. Ben was antsy about it the other day. Asked me to feel Cascadia out about the situation. But he said he didn't want to take sides. In my opinion, it's a bad idea. But we haven't discussed it as a Pack. With things so bad right now, I don't know what to say."

Gabe scrubbed his hands over his face. "I understand your predicament, Nick, I really do. But it is important. For precisely the reasons you bring up. The humans are suspicious of us as it is. This is something I'd like you to look into soon." He sighed.

"Well, this is probably a good time to bring up what I found today." Nina pulled some papers out of a file folder on the low table near the couch. "I did a basic search through the transaction records for the past three years. I looked into Pack accounts and the personal accounts of Sarah and Ben as well."

Nick looked up sharply but said nothing.

"I'm sorry, Nick. I just thought it would be wise to cover all the bases. I looked at yours as well."

"Nina!" Tracy objected. "I didn't ask you to do that."

"I know you didn't. But damn it, you're in danger down there and there will be an accounting. And I don't feel guilty about watching your back, I'm your best friend and big sister and that's what we do. In any case, Nick is all clear. He's a very nice prospect, Trace. He pays his bills on time and has a very nice nest egg. Way to go."

Tracy lost the edge of her anger and rolled her eyes.

"But I can't say the same of Ben and Sarah. Or rather, I can now, but about eighteen months ago things got very tight. They have a nice living. She brings in nearly two hundred grand a year and he pulls in about the same from the Pack. But there'd be times when there was nothing in the account and they were overdrawn. She took out large cash advances on their credit cards until she maxed them out. Then everything was fine for a few months and she'd pay back the credit cards and the accounts and then it would happen again. Only, Pack money began to ebb and flow on her schedule." Nina handed the papers to Nick, who stared at them, shocked.

"And then, about six months after that, huge amounts of money started moving through the Pack accounts. And then payments made to three different companies. Always the same three companies. In really large amounts. I haven't been able to find out much about these companies, though. One is a place that makes plastic. Can't imagine why the Pack would have paid nearly half a million dollars to a company that makes plastic in the last nine months. Can you?"

"I don't know what the hell any of this is." Nick stared at the paperwork in front of him. "I've never heard of any of these companies. They aren't Pack businesses."

"Well, and I don't mean to brag, but I'm pretty slick at finding things out and I hit a major brick wall here on these outfits. They look like fronts and well, naturally my mind jumps to who we all know who runs front businesses."

"You are so bent," Lex murmured, a gleam in his eyes as he spoke to his wife.

"Easy there, Scooby. Let me finish here."

Gabe laughed as Lex snorted before kissing her neck and leaning back to listen.

"Are you saying my Pack is doing business with the mafia?" The anguish in Nick's voice was clear.

"I'm sorry, Nick. Even more specific, I'm saying your brother and his mate appear to be laundering money through the Pack's accounts for the mafia."

"How can you know? You're a gardener!" Nick stood up and began to pace. Lex growled but Nina patted his thigh.

"I am now, yeah. But let's just say I have a colorful past and leave it at that. Enough color to know what this is." Nina looked to Gabe. "Not enough to prove it in a court of law, of course. But common sense can tell you something that you need to back up with months of investigation."

"This can't be happening. Things were so simple a week ago." Nick sat back down.

"It's got to be connected. Pellini is working to expand his power. Damn it! It's hard being away right now. The other wolves in the inner circle are very concerned and I've gotten calls from some of the other Packs I mentioned, they've seen an increase in the presence in certain problems associated with the Pellinis. Just like this one. I need to get back out there and continue to monitor this."

Tracy closed her eyes as guilt speared through her. He was there because of her. If it weren't for her, he'd be back in Boston taking care of business. Nick was going through this because of her presence in his life. She fought back tears of frustration, not wanting to lose it in front of her family.

"Excuse me a moment." Gabe turned to her and took her chin in his hand. "What is it?" His voice was gentle in contrast to his normal voice of address, which was more formal and cool.

Tracy blushed red. "Nothing. God! Don't let me interrupt you." The last thing she wanted was to be a bigger distraction than she was already.

"Don't lie to me. I can feel that you're upset." His eyes bored straight into hers.

"I can feel it, too. Come on, baby, tell us," Nick tried to coax her gently.

"She feels guilty!" Nina said it like any idiot could have figured it out.

"Why on earth would she feel guilty?" Gabe turned back to look at Nina.

"Hello? I'm sitting right here and I've just said I didn't want to interrupt you. Get on with it, we have a lot of stuff to cover."

"Don't get pissy with me, Tracy. I'm not going to say another word until you tell me what the hell is wrong." Gabe loomed over her.

Tracy raised an eyebrow and crossed her arms over her chest. "Pissy? Let's talk about this later. *In private.*"

"What? No. There's obviously something wrong! Talk to me, damn it. Talk to *us*, we're your mates."

"Oh for cripes' sake!" Cade exploded. "Even I can see it and according to Nina I'm a blind jerk. You said that your being here was a problem. You're here because of her. Nick's Pack's business is being uncovered in light of the whole shitstorm from the Pack house the other night. Ergo, she feels like she's responsible in that totally insane way that women have about shit like this."

Gabe got up and dragged Tracy out of the room. "We'll be back in a few minutes," he called over his shoulder. Nick followed.

Milton yawned and padded over to Nina, who leaned back against the couch, absently scratching behind his ears and feeling mildly sorry for Gabe and Nick.

"Well, I suppose a plus of having two males to one female is that you're not the one always on her shit list. Unless you're our sister and manage to be upset with both of them." Lex chuckled.

"Hmm, maybe I need to look for another mate then," Nina shot back and that shut Lex up.

* * * * *

Gabe hauled Tracy downstairs and out onto the back deck overlooking the wilderness behind the house. "First of all, when I hurt your feelings, I'd like it if you told me when I ask you directly. It's not fair of you to be hurt and not let me try and fix it."

"Why do you always have to be so fucking reasonable, Gabe?" Tracy stormed off to the other side of the deck where Nick stood. She sighed and leaned against the rails.

"Why do I have to be reasonable? What kind of question is that? I'm a reasonable man, it's what I do. It's who I am."

Nick moved to stand in front of her. He tipped her chin up with a fingertip. "Baby, I didn't mean to make you feel bad in there. There's plenty of guilt to go around, but none of it is yours. My brother and Sarah have that dubious honor. And me too. I'm the Enforcer and I missed that. You've done nothing wrong. You've been good and loving and strong for me. A true mate and partner."

Gabe spoke, watching her from across the deck, "And yes, I need to get back to Boston but that doesn't mean that you're impeding me. I want to be here with you. I love you. I have a job that makes this complicated and well, the whole tri-mate thing makes it even more difficult to work around, but certainly we will. We will because it's how we'll have to be. In order for this to work we all have to do our part. That means you have to tell us when you're upset and we'll do the same and all of us have to try to accommodate each other." He pushed himself away from the railing and went to her.

Tracy nodded up at him. Nick put his arm around each of their waists. "We'll make this work. One step at a time."

Gabe leaned down and brushed his lips over hers and that familiar fire sparked and caught Nick with a gasp. Suddenly his mouth was hot on her neck, just below her ear, feasting on her hammering pulse.

"Turn around, hands on the railing," Gabe murmured into her ear.

"What? My parents are inside!"

Nick spun her and reached around, unzipping her jeans around her slapping hands. "They're not coming out here, we're making up from a fight. They won't want to interfere. And you were told to do something, Tracy."

"Hey! You can't tell me what to do. This isn't a cave or the Dark Ages!"

Nick leaned in, his body against the long line of her back, while Gabe yanked her jeans and panties down. The cool of the evening caressed the bare skin of her thighs. "But I can. Gabe can. What's more, Tracy, you like it." He reached down and slid his fingertips through her pussy. Finding her slick, he chuckled. "Tell you what, let's be blunt. You like to be dominated and we like dominating you. It won't go past sex, we won't tell you what books to read or who you can go to the movies with."

"But when I tell you to turn and grab something and spread your thighs, you'll do it. And we all know you'll like it." Gabe's lips moved against her ear and the sound of unzipping flies brought a shiver of desire through her and she moaned softly.

"First, I'm going to fuck you. Hard and fast so those sweet breasts jiggle the way I like. Then Gabe's going to fuck you. Your job is to come. A lot." Nick underlined this with a long, hard thrust into her until he slid in to the root.

Gabe ducked under where her hands grasped the railing and faced her. "Now," he said quietly as Nick began to move into her body at her back, "let's get started with your part, shall we?"

He leaned in to kiss her while his hands found her nipples under her sweater. She arched her back, pressing into his palms.

Coherent thought escaped her. She should be scandalized, having sex out on the shadowy deck with her parents in the house behind them. She should be outraged that her mates just ordered her to fuck them. But she wasn't. God, she was turned on beyond all bearing. So turned on she'd have to feel ashamed of herself later because all she had was endorphins racing through her system and pleasure intoxicating her as their hands and mouths were on her and Nick's cock filled her over and over.

Nick reached around and found her clit swollen and slick for him and circled it slowly, ramping up the need, pushing her desire higher and higher. Knowing that someone could walk out at any moment was a dark thrill and her first orgasm slammed into her when Gabe's teeth closed over the tendons in her neck.

Writhing between them as she came, she was only barely cognizant of Nick's climax as his hand at her hip convulsed and her name came as a hoarse sigh from his lips.

Nick pulled out and Gabe picked her up. He sat on one of the Adirondack chairs, putting her on his lap reverse cowgirl. Her body faced away from him and she locked eyes with Nick as Gabe's cock filled her cunt, still fluttering from climax.

Nick knelt before them both and looked into her eyes. "I love you so much, Tracy. You're so beautiful and sexy." Shoving her sweater up, he licked over her nipples until she made soft sounds of entreaty and squirmed against Gabe.

He kissed down her belly and spread her open, exposing her clit. She looked down at him, at the top of his head. His glossy black hair was soft between her fingers as she moved her hands to caress his skull between her palms.

She did feel beautiful and sexy. Loved, cherished and desired. Despite the ugliness of what they'd found out and the uncertainty of that part of the future, she felt assured of her place in the world with these two men at her side. It didn't matter where or how, she just knew, accepted for a certainty that things would be all right because they were meant to be.

Gabe held her hips tight, pressing her down on his cock. He wasn't so much thrusting as circling himself into her, pulsing deep.

Nick certainly knew his way around her pussy. The flat of his tongue slid over her even as Gabe held her tight against him. The dual sensation of being filled with Gabe's cock and Nick's tongue on her clit shocked through her, singeing her senses until she fell into another orgasm.

"Oh, damn, yes. You feel so good, Tracy." Gabe's words were against the back of her neck. Strained, as he worked toward his own end. Which he found some moments later.

He sat there, breath heaving, heart pounding, head against her back, breathing her in. "I'm a lucky wolf, babe.

Sixteen years younger than me, a completely sexy woman and the perfect saucy sub. I love you."

She cracked a smile as he helped her stand and she pulled her pants back up and her sweater back down. "I love you too." She looked to Nick. "And you. God, that was pretty damned hot. But I'm not sure that two orgasms count as coming a lot." She raised a brow at them.

Gabe gave a surprised laugh as he pulled her to him. "You're correct. We'll rectify that when we get home."

"Now, let's go back inside and finish all of this up." Nick held out a hand and she took it.

"Of course, we reek of sex. God." Her face was hot.

Nick grinned. "The ones who're mated will understand. The ones who aren't will be envious."

Chapter Seven

ஐ

The next morning, refreshed from make-up sex and a nice run in the woods behind Cade's house, their first since bonding, they woke up and got working.

Her sisters and Nina came over to supervise the movers while Tracy went to the store to talk with Charity, who was thrilled by the idea of running Spin the Black Circle full-time for her while she was in Portland. She also encouraged Tracy to open another store there.

Some hours later they'd handed over the keys to Tegan and had loaded Milton into Tracy's Outback and they were all heading back south for the meeting later that day with Ben.

They stopped by the new house, which Milton heartily approved of, especially the addition of a doggie door just his size that led into the back yard, and were there for the delivery of the new bedroom furniture that Tracy ordered for the master bedroom. She'd brought over the clothes from her house and some of Nick's and Gabe's as well. Between Tracy's stuff from her house and what Nick had and some things Gabe would have shipped, the house would have plenty of furniture.

For the time being, they decided to all share a bedroom. They all wanted to sleep against each other every night. Nick would have an office of his own on the first floor and Gabe would have one just off the master bedroom.

Tracy didn't need one, if she set up a shop she'd do the books at home but her laptop could go anywhere.

It came up on six and they ate, showered and got in the car to drive to the Pack house. Nick consulted with Josh, the

Third, and some of the other guards who would all be there to get his back if need be.

Tracy was nervous as hell. She wanted very badly for this to work out. Nick had asked to be allowed to deal with the money laundering suspicions his own way and Gabe and Tracy agreed.

It was only the inner circle that night, the Alpha pair, the Second through Fifth and Tracy and Gabe as Nick's mates and Seconds. Nick and Ben's parents were there as well, as the retired Alpha pair.

When they entered the room Sarah narrowed her eyes at Tracy, who sent her a mental *fuck off* but ignored her.

Until she spoke. "He is not welcome at this meeting." Meaning Gabe.

"On the contrary. As he is part of the tri-mate bond, he is also Second here. He shares my status as much as Tracy does." Nick didn't raise his voice or show any emotion. He sat down and Tracy sat to one side, Gabe to the other. There was no inclination of the head.

"All we have is your word about that," Sarah sneered and Tracy growled.

"Yes, well, some of us can be trusted." Gabe looked at her with disdain. "In any case, everyone here who is a wolf knows the truth. You can all scent it. I'm not arguing it with you."

"How dare you speak to her that way?" Ben growled at Gabe.

Nick held up a hand and touched Gabe's arm slightly to stay him. "He merely spoke the truth. Do not raise your voice to him again. Let's get moving with this, I don't want any of my time wasted." Tracy looked at Nick, his eyes were hard, mouth set. He emanated strength and menace. It made her all tingly to watch.

"Fine. I demand an apology from you and your mates. Both of them. And I want it in front of the Pack. I want to see obedience from you in the future."

Tracy fought the urge to burst out laughing. This was serious for many reasons and it was Nick's family, she didn't want this to hurt him any more than it had to.

"Try again." Nick's face was still an impassive mask.

Ben paled a bit and Sarah sat forward in her chair. "Nick, how can you turn your back on your family like this? Can't you see that she's manipulating you? She's making you betray your Pack. And for what? A scrawny piece of ass?"

Nick's eyes went that otherworldly blue and a deep growl trickled from his lips. The hair on the back of Tracy's neck rose and she grabbed his hand. "She's goading you," Tracy murmured.

"She should be aware that I have no patience left in this matter. She should be aware that people with a modicum of intelligence and craft can look into bank accounts and see some very irregular things. She should be aware that *she* has betrayed this Pack and with the aid of her mate, a man I used to be proud to call Alpha and brother." Nick's voice had gone emotionless again. He was almost a different man like this. A machine. A big fucking scary bad wolf who was interested in the truth and nothing more.

"What did you say?" Josh demanded.

"Nick?" Their mother looked at him, confused.

"I think Ben and Sarah should tell you all what they've been up to."

Ben had the good grace to look ashamed but Sarah's face was an angry mask. "I don't need to defend myself against stupid accusations. Jealous accusations. She wants to be Alpha, Nick, and you're handing it to her!"

Nick looked at her and shook his head. "Ben? Come on, just admit it. It has to be wearing on you. I can't believe you'd get behind this purely for profit. Be a leader, own up to what you did." Nick's eyes held a light of tenderness.

"I don't know what you're talking about, Nick. I think Sarah is right and Tracy has turned you against your own family. It breaks my heart but I fear I'm going to have to sever your ties to Pacific."

Several gasps filled the room and Tracy wanted to leap over there and punch Ben Lawrence in the nose. Arrogant, lying asshole! How dare they call her mate a liar! She felt how it tore him up inside to deal with this betrayal.

Bending, Nick opened the case at his feet and tossed a file to Josh. "It's all there. Sarah and Ben have been using the Pack to launder cash for the Pellini Group. This has been going on for nearly a year."

Despite the appearance of a lack of emotion, Tracy felt his inner turmoil. She and Gabe both moved a bit closer to him, trying to lend him some comfort with their presence.

The Fourth, who had been solidly on Ben's side, and the Fifth moved in close to Josh to look at the papers while Ben and Nick's parents stared, shocked, at Sarah and Ben.

Sarah jumped up and tried to grab the paperwork but Ben intercepted her and yanked her down beside him.

After a few minutes of silent reading, the others all looked up to stare in disbelief at their Alpha pair.

Nick sat, solid and unmoving. His muscles were tight and his jaw was clenched. Tracy ached for him and caught Gabe's eye and saw he was worried too. But she knew if she touched him or tried to overtly comfort him it would weaken his position. Right then he was the face of justice for the Pack. It was his job as Enforcer to see that right was done.

"Ben, I think it's time you told the truth. Why would you do this? You've endangered us all with your association with the Pellini Group. You've betrayed your position as Alpha. Your job is to protect this Pack but you've turned your back, abandoned your responsibilities to your wolves." Nick stood and took the papers back and looked at Ben and Sarah, waiting.

"I don't know what you're talking about! It's all lies!" Sarah jumped at Tracy, who stood and moved to the side, knocking her fist into Sarah's temple.

"Stand down!" Ben stood, screaming. Nick pushed him back into his chair.

"You stand down, Ben. Be a fucking man! Own this or I'll have to end it my way."

Tracy's foot was on Sarah's throat. "Don't even think of getting up. I *will* challenge you, and you and I both know how that'll end up."

"Okay! Just let her go, damn it. I'll tell you everything."

Tracy looked back at Nick, who waited a long moment before nodding shortly. She removed her foot but growled, "Don't piss me off any more tonight, Sarah. Now go sit the fuck down."

"How dare you?" Sarah spat as she started to stand.

"Sarah, for god's sake, shut up!" Ben thundered and they all turned to look at him in surprise. "You're making this worse." Chastened and a bit shocked, she went to him and sat down at his side.

"Sarah was in trouble with work. She'd overextended herself and had used client money in a way she wasn't supposed to." He told them of the dance she'd done, shuffling money around until she was facing jail and had no choice but to go to Pellini. He'd been looking through the Pack statement three months back and had gotten the shock of his life. When he confronted her, the whole story spilled out.

"I was trying to find a way out of this mess but you mated with the one family Pellini hates more than any other! Don't you see, it's her, it's Tracy. She's the problem. If she hadn't come along we'd still be friends. We'd still be a family." Sarah's voice was a whine by that point and Tracy ached to knock the shit out of her.

"This is all you!" Nick screamed so loud that Tracy jumped and Ben's nose started to bleed. "You've done this to our family. You've betrayed us all with your fucking greed. Damn you! You've ruined my brother. You've betrayed all the feelings I ever had for you. You've turned him into something that disgusts me. He's turned his back on what is right for you and you *dare* to blame Tracy? Do you have *any* idea the situation you've placed me in?"

Sarah was crying in earnest and Ben's eyes were closed at the realization. "Just let me fix this, Nicky," she sobbed.

Josh reached out to touch Tracy's arm when she made a move at the use of the endearment. He shook his head subtly. She knew, she knew, but oh how she wanted to take that bitch down.

"Don't. You're nothing to me now and the only reason you're still breathing at all is because of my niece and nephew."

"Nick, let's focus for a moment on what we need to do here," his father said. "You're within your rights to challenge Ben. But that won't change this fuck-up. I've just lost a son in many ways, I'd prefer not to lose him all the way. I'm asking you for mercy on his behalf. Not because he deserves to lead this Pack, he doesn't. But because he's my son and your brother and the father of my grandchildren." He turned to Tracy. "We've wronged you. I apologize for that. You're also within your rights to challenge Sarah and I know you'd win and she does too. So I guess I'm asking you for your mercy too. Again, not because she deserves it. I'm ashamed of her and what she's done to this Pack and my son. But she has children and those children need a mother."

Josh shook his head. "And what are you proposing? That we just all turn a blind eye to this? Their forsaking of their oaths as Alpha because they have kids? I'm sorry, Charles, but I can't get behind that."

"Stop talking about us like we're not here!" Sarah exclaimed.

"Shut up," Gabe ordered. And she did, reminding him once again, that Sarah and Ben were not fit to be Alphas of Pacific Pack. "You have no idea what you've done, have you? You never should have been Alpha, neither of you. Stupid. So fucking stupid. Do you realize what Warren Pellini is? What he's capable of? And you've given him the keys to the front door of this Pack. The Pack where your children live, damn you. You're going to fix it? How's that? Do you think he'll just let you walk away after you've laundered half a million dollars for him? With all you know?

"Normally I'd counsel you to go to the National Enforcer. Except he's in Pellini's pocket too. There's no system in place to protect you *because* of Warren Pellini. There is no *fixing it*, Sarah. You're fucked and you've dragged your entire Pack down with you. All for money. I hope it was worth the lives of everyone you were supposed to be caring for."

"What do we do, then?" Ben leaned forward, wiping the blood from his nose on his sleeve.

"You're unfit to lead this Pack. You will step down and take Sarah with you. Nick should have been Alpha all this time. I shouldn't have kept my mouth closed about it," Nick's mother said quietly.

Ben flinched but nodded. "You're right. I'm sorry. God. So sorry. But I still want to help. This mess is our fault, I want to help clean it up. I still love this Pack."

"Ben! You can't just give in to this. They're all crazy. Pellini can help us. He can help us keep control here. He'll send people, he told me."

Ben turned on her, despair in his eyes. "What? Sarah, what have you become? You want to sic thugs on our family? You want them to infiltrate this Pack even more than they already have? My god, I'm sick with this. I'm sick because I'm bound to you and you used to be something so much more and now you're rotten on the inside. And I don't know how to be quit of this connection to you." He put his head in his hands and wept.

Tracy moved to Gabe's side, sitting on the arm of his chair. She desperately wanted to go to Nick but he had to do this on his own, handle it his way.

"I don't think it's necessary to challenge Ben, do you?" Gabe spoke quietly to Nick. "Ascend, it's your birthright. Tracy will sit at your right hand like a real Alpha female."

Nick turned to him. "And you at my left hand. Three Alphas to rule this Pack. I won't ask you to turn away from National, your job is very important. But if I'm Alpha, so are you, just as Tracy is."

"Stop talking about this like it's going to happen. I'm not giving it up," Sarah snarled.

"Stop talking crazy, Sarah. You don't have a chance in hell of winning a challenge against Tracy and you know it. You'll be dead, and what about Chris and Haley then? Are you such a callous mother that your greed surpasses that too? When did this happen to you? How could I have missed the change?" Nick just looked at her with disgust on his face.

Nick stood and began to pace. "No. As of this moment, I am Alpha of Pacific. Your ties, along with Ben's, are severed. You are shunned. You have a few hours to get your stuff and leave. I'll allow you to take ten thousand dollars to start a new life elsewhere. You'll have to lay low for a while."

Ben stood and went to his brother. "I am so sorry, Nick. Please, let me help you. He won't just leave you alone. He told Sarah that he's got evidence on the Pack that he'll turn over to the National Enforcer if she tries to back out."

Nick looked at Ben for long moments and the two of them embraced. Tracy's heart ached for Nick. If Lex or Cade ever did something that betrayed Cascadia, she couldn't imagine the betrayal she'd feel. But they'd still be her brothers and she'd still love them.

Ben went to his knees and lowered his head in obeisance to Nick and Nick put his hand out to touch his shoulder. Tracy felt whatever magic that bound an Alpha to a Pack slam into her. Felt the responsibility of all her wolves nestle in her soul. It was heavy, but it felt right too. She turned and looked at Gabe, who blinked slowly and then relaxed back into his chair, and she knew it had happened to him as well. She wondered how he would deal with the dual responsibilities he'd hold as Third in National and Alpha in Pacific. What a complicated road he faced.

Sarah jumped off the couch with a scream and lunged at Tracy, who tossed her to the side. "I won't! You can't lead, they won't follow you! This is my Pack!"

"No. It's my Pack now. You don't deserve them. Don't move, Sarah. I'm not your anchor and I don't like you. You disgust me and I have no compunction about taking you down in a challenge. As far as I'm concerned, your children would be better off without you."

Nick flinched and Ben gasped. Keeping Sarah in her line of vision, Tracy addressed them. "What? Do I lie? Tell me. Because someone had better well start leading this Pack because it's not happening. Pacific is a disgrace. Why didn't your accountant come to Nick? As Enforcer, it was something he should have been told. But this Pack has been rudderless for how long now? Even now, this bitch has betrayed you all, has attacked me and still you're making excuses? Lead or get out of the way because I am Alpha and I am willing to do what it takes to get Warren Pellini and his family out of our business. And if you think that's going to happen because we ask nicely, you're out of your fucking minds. And Sarah, if you get up off that floor I will kill you without breaking a sweat, I mean it. Don't look to Nick to save you, he couldn't reach me in time to stop me."

"They won't follow you!" Sarah sniveled.

Josh stood and knelt next to Ben. "I swear my fealty to you, Alpha, and your mates."

The Fourth and Fifth followed suit and Gabe raised a brow at Tracy and flicked a dispassionate glance in Sarah's direction. "Looks like you were wrong."

"Get up." Nick motioned to the wolves who'd gone to their knees.

"What about my children? Nicky, will you just toss your niece and nephew out into the street?"

"Don't call me that. We'd be happy to keep Chris and Haley here or up with Cascadia until this is solved. We'll keep them safe. They are my blood and my Pack. I love them and want to keep them safe. But they're not going to save you."

"Call her off!"

"No." Nick turned to Tracy. "It's up to her." Turning again, he looked at Gabe. "Let's start working on a plan to deal with Pellini."

"Not in her presence. I don't trust her." Gabe nodded his head toward Sarah. "In fact, I don't trust her not to go running to Pellini the first moment she can."

"We'll take her up to our vacation house in eastern Oregon. The kids are on midwinter break from school anyway, they can come too. Keep it quiet and low-key," Nick's mother said.

"They might know to look there. Hang on a second." Tracy pulled out her cell phone and called Lex.

"Lex, I need some help."

Without any other questions he agreed immediately. "What do you need, sweetie?"

Tracy smiled. "I need one of the cabins on the Peninsula and a few of your guards." She briefed him quickly on the situation. He agreed to send three of his guards out to the cabin to wait for the arrival of Nick's parents, Sarah and the kids and however many guards Nick wanted to have accompany them. He told her to call if she needed anything else and reminded her to stay safe.

"I suppose Josh is Enforcer now. Send two men you trust absolutely out with my parents and Sarah and the kids. Don't let Sarah near a phone. Do not let her go anywhere alone. Cooperate with the Cascadia guards. Our lives are on the line here. Shoot her in the head if she tries to contact *anyone* but me or Ben." Nick looked at his friend, who took up the responsibility immediately and went into action.

Nick's father embraced him. "You're going to do a fine job, son. Let us know if you need anything. We'll get out of here as soon as we can."

Ben went to Sarah and hugged her but she yelled at him to stop Nick. He shook his head. "No. I'm going to do what's right by this Pack and by our children. Please don't make trouble. We can rebuild our lives somewhere else when this is over. You know it's what we have to do."

"You have to do right by me, Ben! We can go and be part of the Pellini Group! He'll take us in."

"You're delusional. He'll kill you and the kids. He's a murderer and a thug. Please go. I'm begging you to cooperate and behave."

Once the others had left holding a defeated-looking Sarah, Nick turned back to Ben. "Here's what we're going to do. Nothing. Not for a bit anyway. How often does he contact Sarah?"

"Once every two weeks or so. He did his last exchange a week ago so you have a bit of time. What do you have in mind? I offered to buy him out but he just laughed. Said he was making way more through the Pack than I could pay him."

Nick's jaw tightened. "Why didn't you come to me? Damn it, I'm your brother, I would have helped."

"I was scared and ashamed. I wanted to fix it before anyone found out. I was wrong, I know that."

"We'll go to Boston. Introduce Tracy to National. I'll have to get a special dispensation to keep my position there and here too." Gabe tapped his bearded chin as he spoke. "The Enforcer will be there. I need to feel him out on this. I wanted to wait but it's too late, it needs to happen now. If wolves can't count on the protection of the National Pack, what good are we? He's really not a bad man, just arrogant."

Tracy snorted. *How uncommon for a high-ranking male wolf.* Not. "Seems to me this is a three-tiered issue. First, how do we get them out of Pack business? We can't just say no at this stage or he'll use the information and destroy us. Secondly, we need to figure out a way to make the kids safe. And they won't be as long as Pellini sees Sarah as his way in and thinks we can be persuaded by harming the kids. Lastly, the problem of the Pellini Group as a whole and their connection to the National Enforcer."

Suddenly she asked, "Gabe, is he unmated?"

Gabe narrowed his eyes at her. "Yes, but you're not single."

She rolled her eyes and waved him off. "Duh."

"What are you up to?"

"Answer the question."

"Yes. He's straight and unmated but you're not going to tear off on some half-formed plan to seduce him over to our side."

Narrowing her eyes at him, she growled. "Don't you talk to me like I'm some stupid piece of fluff, Gabe Murphy. I am an intelligent woman who is the Alpha of this Pack. I demand respect, especially from my mate."

He stood and went to her, getting in her face. "I will protect you at any cost. Even if your feelings get in a snit."

"You are an asshole, Gabe." Spinning, she addressed Nick, who hid his dismay. "If he's unmated it'll be three against one. He doesn't stand a chance against all of us. And each of us has our own area of power. You're a former Enforcer and now an Alpha, I know inner circle well, my family is a ruling family too. And Gabe, while utterly a prick right now, is the Mediator. He won't know what hit him."

Nick's eyebrows went up and he grinned, nodding. "Excellent idea, baby."

"We'll call and get the travel arrangements made when we get back home."

"You can call from here. It's your house now that you're the Alpha," Ben said quietly. "Tracy, I'm very sorry. I panicked and blamed it all on you. I know it's not your fault. I am happy Nick found you."

"I don't want to live here. No offense. But Cade doesn't live in the Pack house either and runs Cascadia just fine. The Pack ate my father alive and nearly destroyed my parents' marriage because they had no distance. I don't want that. Nick doesn't want to live here and I'm with him on that." She paused and put her hands in her pockets. "As for your apology, as I told Sarah, actions speak louder than words, Ben. I hope you're telling the truth. Mostly for Nick's sake because he loves you. Keep in mind that I don't and I'll do whatever it takes to protect him and this Pack."

"I respect that. The news is going to spread that you're all Alpha now. How do you deal with that when Pellini hears? Sarah called him, freaked out about Tracy. He knows there're problems."

"Damn woman! Well, let's not hide that. Ben will still be seen around. Make it seem that the Ascension was amicable. For now let's leave Sarah's name on the accounts. She can't do anything from the cabin anyway. Ben, keep her phone so when Warren calls, you can cover for Sarah's absence. Assure him that everything is fine and that you're still doing the accounts."

"You sure that's wise? Letting Ben talk to Pellini?" Josh asked.

"I'm going to trust my brother, Josh. He knows that not only is his life at stake but also the lives of his kids, who'll never be safe until we get Pellini out of this Pack."

Josh took a deep breath and nodded.

"Let's get an announcement made and set up a Howl. We'll get out to Boston tomorrow and deal then. We'll do the

Howl when we get back." Nick pulled on the mantle of leadership easily and Tracy knew he was born to it. "We're going home. I'll keep in touch, Josh. Do what you need to to keep the Pack safe in my absence."

"I'll send two guards with you when you travel to Boston. An Alpha has the right to travel with guards, especially into another territory. And I insist on you having two guards live at your new place. You're the Alpha triad now, you need the protection."

Gabe nodded. "That's acceptable. I'll contact the Enforcer's office and make the arrangements."

Nick knew he'd have insisted on the same thing and nodded. "Fine. Send Derek and Trey over."

They went back out to the car and Tracy got behind the wheel to drive back to the house. Gabe tried to catch Tracy's eye but she wasn't having it. He knew there'd be hell to pay for his comments earlier. And he had to admit, he deserved it. He jumped to conclusions, she waved them off and he'd charged at her again, assuming the worst.

Back at home, they got out and showed Derek and Trey where the room downstairs that was to have been Nick's office was. "You can bunk in here for now. We'll clear out the study tomorrow so each of you can have your own room."

They nodded at Tracy and she smiled and went upstairs. Gabe was waiting in the office just off the master suite. Ignoring him, she moved around his body and grabbed the phone to call Nina, explaining the basics and asking her to keep an eye out for anything hinky with the National Enforcer's accounts.

Without looking at Gabe, she spoke coolly, "You need to get the permission to travel taken care of so I can get the plane situation taken care of."

He grabbed her but she remained stiff in his arms. "Tracy, I'm sorry."

She remained silent.

Sighing, he tried another tack. "I should have trusted you. I underestimated you and I'm sorry."

"You thought I'd whore myself?"

Jerking in surprise, he held her body out so he could look into her face. "What? I never said any such thing!"

"Oh really? And what was your *assumption*? Hmmm? You assumed that I was going to seduce the Enforcer over to our side, did you not? Like a whore. Well, fuck you, Gabe. I don't need to sell my pussy to figure this."

He paled. "I… Jesus, Tracy, I didn't mean it that way. I'm sorry. It sounds that way, yes. But I'd never think that of you." Leaning in, he brushed his lips over hers and she relaxed in his arms. "I'm sorry, honey. I hate that I hurt your feelings."

She looked up into his eyes and smiled softly. "I hate it too. And I accept your apology."

Sitting on the desk, he pulled her to stand between his thighs. "You know, it's been forever since I've been inside you."

She laughed. "It's been six hours."

"Okay, so it's been longer than I want. Go to Nick and I'll get permission and make the plane reservations and call my assistant to have my house readied for us all. I'll be in in a bit."

Moving in tight against his body, she captured his bottom lip between her teeth. "Okay. See you in a few minutes."

On her way out, he swatted her ass and she flipped him off over her shoulder. His laugh delighted her and the tension and anger were gone.

But her concern wasn't. She'd given Nick a bit of time but it was enough and she wanted to go to him. She felt his pain as she walked into the bedroom. He sat on the chaise near the French doors leading to the veranda, absently stroking a hand over Milton's head. Milton was really good at cheering people up, goodness knows she'd snuggled up to him plenty enough over the last four years.

"Hey," she said quietly as she moved toward him.

"Everything okay between you and Gabe?"

"Yes. But don't worry about that. How are you? I'm so sorry you had to go through that tonight." She stood behind him, putting her arms around his shoulders to hug him.

"Never in a million years did I ever imagine having to shun my brother and Sarah from the Pack." His voice was thick with emotion.

"You did the right thing. And you know, Ben is going to help, which makes a huge difference. He obviously can't stay, the Pack won't trust him. But he can start over somewhere else, either in another Pack or on their own without the shame. He can raise his children with pride. Everyone makes mistakes, Nick. And where character lies is how we deal with them. We can run like Sarah, or face it head-on like Ben. You faced it, Nick. You did the hard thing. It's what Alphas do."

He turned, standing and pulling her to him. "You understand me. I've never thought it was important, really, to be understood. But always in the back of my mind it hurt that no one did."

"I love you, Nick. I know you and I love you." She went up on her toes and kissed his chin. "I believe in you." A kiss to the hollow of his throat as her hands pulled his shirt from his pants. Leaning back, she yanked it over his head and tossed it behind her.

The warmth of his skin nearly burned her palms as she slid them up the wall of his chest. His scent hit her in the face and wrapped itself around her, pulling her to him physically and emotionally.

She laid a series of openmouthed kisses over his collarbone, tongue flicking out to taste the salt of his skin. His breathing sped, pulse hammering under her lips.

Moving back to the bed, he spun to push her onto the mattress and loomed above her. She shook her head and rolled, coming to straddle his waist. Putting a finger over his lips, she said, "Shhh. Let me love you, Nick."

His eyes lit with emotion then and he kissed the finger that had quieted him. And she went back to work. Back to the slow, sensual exploration of every inch of his face and neck with her lips. She poured every bit of her love for him into those kisses.

Scooting down his body, she looked up into his eyes as she kissed a path over to each nipple, grazing her teeth over each one and delighting in his shiver of pleasure and low gasp. Down she went, her hands working to undo his jeans, and once her mouth reached the sensitive spot just below his belly button she sat up long enough to pull the rest of his clothes off.

Kneeling between his thighs, she gazed up his body. "You're so beautiful. God, no wonder every woman in Pacific hated me on sight. This is mine, all mine and I'm so not going to share." She chuckled and he smiled up at her with cocky arrogance and assuredness of his own allure.

She slid her hands up his thighs, over those tight muscles, and felt them loosen under her touch. Each moment she loved him with her hands and mouth, she felt the tension and the hurt fall away a bit more.

Finally, she leaned down and grazed his cock with her cheek, stopping for a moment to breathe him in. The scent of fully aroused werewolf male rode her, tightened her gut and made her pussy slick. Her clit throbbed and her nipples hardened to the point of near pain. Mate called to mate then and each gave a small sigh of desire and satisfaction.

Her ass swaying, she bent down and took him into her mouth, slowly drawing her tongue 'round and 'round the head of his cock as she did. In slow but sure rhythm, she went down on him, drawing his cock into her mouth as far as she could and then pulling back up, making sure to flick her tongue over him as she pulled all the way off. She knew he was watching and gave him a show.

His balls were in her palms and she felt them pull up toward his body as he neared climax. Her entire focus was on bringing him pleasure and she drowned in his response. All she could feel, see, hear and taste was Nick.

Her skull was cradled between his hands, his grip guiding her movements as his hips began to roll to meet her mouth.

When he came, her name was a benediction from his lips. He poured his love for her into that sound as she took his pleasure into her body.

She found herself being picked up and pulled against Gabe, her back to Gabe's front, her head turned to receive his kiss while Nick practically ripped her shirt off.

Big hands pulled her pants and panties off and Gabe still held her, her head tipped back on his shoulder as Nick pressed his face into her pussy.

"You have no idea how sexy you looked from my vantage point," Gabe murmured in her ear. She gasped as Nick's tongue flicked over her clit. "You have the loveliest ass, babe. I watched you there, swaying as you took Nick into your mouth over and over. My cock is so hard I could drive spikes with it. But you know what I'd rather do?"

There were no words, just a whimper.

Both men chuckled and Nick pulled away and lay back on the bed. She cried out at the loss of his mouth.

"All in due time, honey. Tonight is the night. Nick and I both. Get started while I get out of my clothes." Gently, he put her on Nick, who brought her face to his.

Sensing her apprehension, Nick kissed over her eyelids, his hands slowly caressing her back. "There aren't words to tell you how much you mean to me," he said, lips just barely touching hers. "I believe in you too. This is going to be good, baby. Trust me. Trust Gabe."

"Ride him, honey." Gabe got on the bed and crawled to them.

Taking a deep, fortifying breath, she looked down. Seeing the light in Nick's eyes brought a smile to her lips. Following the line of his body, her smile widened further. No recovery time. Nick was hard and ready to go again. "Such a stud," she said with a laugh.

"For you."

Raising a brow, she sat up and moved back. Reaching behind herself, she grabbed his cock, guided him to her gate and slid back, sinking slowing onto him. The shock of his entry sent shocks of pleasure skittering up her spine as her pussy pulled him in deep.

Nick looked up at her and wondered at her beauty. The rawness of her sexuality was a siren song and he happily cast himself on the rocks. He wanted her, every inch of her. Forever. And in every way he could have her as many times as he could get her.

He watched her alert eyes blur a bit as he filled her. Her lips were swollen from going down on him and wet from his kisses. She was utterly gorgeous.

Gabe knelt behind her, his cock hard and scorching at her back. He kissed down her neck and his hands slid around to her breasts, fingers rolling and pinching her nipples.

Nick watched and wet his fingers, moving them to her clit. He caught sight of Gabe putting a condom on and then lube over the latex-covered head of his cock. Nick's own jumped in response as he pumped into his fist a few times. When Gabe's eyes moved to Nick's an arc of electric attraction shot between them.

But Gabe's attention went back to Tracy as he traced down her back and over the crease in her ass. She tensed and Gabe leaned in. "Shhh. Relax. You have to relax." Slippery fingers stroked over the star of her rear passage and she knew from the bit of play they'd engaged in before that it wasn't an altogether unpleasant experience. "That's it, sweetness."

His fingers slowly worked their way inside her, scissoring to stretch her. She squirmed back against him with small noises of pleasure.

Nick's fingertips stroked over her clit just enough to keep her dancing on the edge of orgasm, and he was close himself from the way her pussy clutched him. She was so wet and hot that there were times he found himself needing to grind his teeth and recite the table of elements to keep from coming.

"Lean back against me now, honey." Gabe moved closer and she leaned her upper body against his chest as he put the head of his cock where his fingers had been a few moments before.

A sound from deep inside her and low in her gut trickled from between her lips as he slowly pressed inside. The feeling was totally overwhelming. Full. Extraordinarily good and on the verge of bad too. Impaled, yeah, that was the word.

"Oh fuck," Gabe mumbled as he finally seated himself fully.

"Yeah. Move it along, Gabe, because I'm half a second from blowing here."

Tracy laughed into a gasp as Gabe pulled out slowly and pressed in again. On his next stroke into her, Nick lifted her and rolled his hips away, pulling out.

The only thing holding her back from screaming at the intensity of feeling were her fingernails digging into her thighs. The way their cocks bumped each other as one pushed in and the other pulled out was maddeningly good. So good it made her delirious.

"Oh yeah, that's it. You're so damned tight." Gabe's words were little more than a grunt.

A mewl broke from her lips as Nick's fingertips intensified their pressure on her clit. "I don't know if I can do this," she gasped. The feelings were so deep, so intense and compelling that they frightened her. Self-control slipped through her fingers as she went spinning into a rush of pleasure greater than she'd ever experienced before.

"Baby, let go. We're here to catch you," Nick said softly.

And she did. And climax broke over her almost violently as her entire body shook with the impact of the intense pleasure. Her head shot back onto Gabe's shoulder and she made a sound close to a wail as the waves of feeling rode her, buffeted her, pulled her under and left her in a place where she could only receive.

Receive the cocks that were pressing into her. Receive the emotions both her mates were broadcasting. Receive the love in the room and the sweat and come and caresses of mouths and hands. Receive the sounds of Nick's and Gabe's climaxes coming, the spasms of cocks and thrusting of muscles until there was nothing left to do but fall in a tangle of arms and legs onto the bed, utterly boneless.

She mumbled something into the pillow and Milton barked and jumped on the bed when Gabe got up.

A sloppy, wet kiss from Milton revived her into a laugh. Rolling a bit back into Nick's body, she scratched right under Milton's chin in the way he liked best. "Well, wow," she said to no one in particular.

Nick laughed behind her and reached around to pet the top of Milton's head. "Yeah, that'll do."

"You like Milty! I knew it." Craning her neck, she looked back at him and he gave her a rueful smile.

"For a three-legged dog, he's not half bad. But he can't sleep in our bed. I draw the line there."

Gabe snorted as he came into the room. "The dog has a bed nearly as nice as ours and a doggie door just his size leading into the backyard. He doesn't need our bed."

"He needs a good foundation to sleep on!" Tracy said, sitting up to kiss Milton's head. He gave a doggie groan of happiness and then, knowing the direction of the conversation, hopped down and went over to his bed and got in it, grinning up at the three of them before closing his eyes.

"So what time do we need to get out of here tomorrow?" Tracy snuggled down between them, breathing in that intoxicating combination of sex and male and wolf.

"National is sending a plane for us at ten. And yes, I made arrangements for Milton to come along too."

Tracy grinned at him from beneath her lashes. "I love that about you. You have this air of untouchable old school about you but beneath that, you're a big old softie." She smirked. "Okay, well, where I'm concerned anyway. Where others are concerned, you're a hardass and that's so sexy. Like I'm the only one who gets to see the sweet, furry underbelly."

"I'm not sure if I should take that as a compliment or not."

Tracy snorted a laugh. "Of course you should. The both of you are all scary big bad wolf business, but with me you're sweet and considerate. I like that very, very much. Makes me feel deliciously girly. But if you tell anyone that I'll deny it."

Nick barked out a surprised laugh and kissed the top of her head. "It's nice to have one area my life where I can let my guard down, you know? A soft, beautiful woman to bury my cock in, to share my troubles with, who has my back."

"Oh yeah. Babe, that bit tonight when you took Sarah out? Wow," Gabe growled and rolled his cock into her side.

She grinned at him. "You liked that? I wanted to rip her fucking head off her neck for talking to Nick that way. I'm sorry, sweetie, I know this has to be hard for you." She turned to Nick.

"Oh, no. Gabe's right. I wanted to turn and rip your jeans off and fuck you right there, even in the midst of all that turmoil. When you're all Alpha like that? Seriously sexy. And when you get jealous?" He shivered and she fluttered her lashes.

Chapter Eight

೫

The plane ride was relatively painless. Milton got to ride in the cabin with them because it was a private plane and he immediately charmed the flight attendant, who kept sneaking him treats.

A car met them at the airport and drove them to Gabe's home in the Back Bay.

"But where do you all run? I can't imagine you all changing and galloping through the Boston Commons under the moon."

"Believe it or not, there's quite a bit of wilderness within a half an hour from here. We can't be as spontaneous as you all can back in the Northwest, but we urban wolves get by." He winked.

Tracy took in the sights as they drove past them. She loved Boston already. It was so beautiful. So much history juxtaposed with modern glass buildings, wide-open parks and close-built neighborhoods. It was so many things at once.

Like Gabe's home, which was actually a condo in a building overlooking the water. "Don't worry, honey, the Pack owns the building and dogs are welcome. If we can't walk Milton, my assistant will be happy to."

Tracy sighed at how wonderful he was.

Yep, impressive all right. When she walked into the giant open front foyer it fairly screamed out old-world elegance. Tall vases flanked the large double doors and she tried not to stare at it all openmouthed like a bumpkin.

A tall woman glided into view and smiled at Gabe. "You're here. Welcome home." She approached and kissed his cheek. But before Tracy could get annoyed, the woman turned to her and grinned. "You must be Tracy. I'm so pleased to meet you! I'm Julie, Gabe's assistant. Please come in. I've prepared the master suite for you."

With that, Julie swept her into a hug filled with genuine warmth.

Milton barked and Julie looked down at him and put her hands on her hips. "And you must be Milton. I'm pleased to meet you as well. Gabe told me all about you and I can't wait to get to know you better. I've even got a bed for you all made. But for now, do you want to go on a walk?"

"Oh that's all right. I can take him. It's not necessary for you to do that."

"Really, it's my pleasure. I love dogs but my mate is allergic. I know, makes me laugh too, considering. But he is. So I'd love to spoil Milton a little when I can."

"Okay, well, thank you. I appreciate that very much."

Julie winked, grabbed Milton's leash and headed outside.

"She's something else."

"She's a wonderful assistant. Pretty much did everything for me. I used to think she was the perfect wife. Took care of my dry cleaning, ordered in the food and no strings other than a paycheck. Now, of course, I see all the other, very fine benefits," he added quickly.

"Let's get settled in. We're to meet with the inner circle this evening. I'm betting there's food in the kitchen."

Gabe led them through the large, two-story apartment, and as the tour continued, Tracy continued to be impressed. The entire place looked out over the sparkling water and across the river lay Cambridge. The place was furnished with beautiful antiques.

"Gabe, this is all really lovely. I feel sort of guilty for bringing you to Portland now."

He stopped and pulled her to him. "This is a nice place, yes. Beautiful view, expensive furniture. All very lovely. But what I have with you in Portland is a home. Stuff can never compare to what I feel here," he put his hand over his heart. "What I have here is a nice place to sleep between working and traveling."

"You travel a lot?" Nick rummaged through the giant Sub-Zero fridge and began to pull out food for a meal. He put a bottle of juice into Tracy's hand and gave her a look that dared her to refuse to drink it. She actually considered it just to see what sort of delicious response it might garner but the discussion was still very serious.

Gabe sighed and pulled out plates. "Yes. I travel out of state at least twice a month for a few days each time."

Tracy barely held back a gasp. The thought of only being with him a week out of the month actually caused her physical pain. In between his travel and his responsibilities to the National Pack, realistically, he'd only be in Portland a week or so at a time, maybe once a month or six weeks with that schedule. The reality of his dual roles hit her hard. It sucked.

Gabe looked at her with narrowed eyes.

Nick turned to her, put a slice of lasagna on her plate and popped it into the microwave. "You're going to eat. You didn't eat any breakfast and you haven't been eating right the last week. When I was checking out your ass this morning I noticed your pants were really loose."

"I'm fine. I just lose my appetite when I'm stressed."

Gabe scowled at her and slathered a huge amount of butter on the bread in his hand. "Eat this."

She took it from him, ate it and tried not to moan at the taste. "Ohmigod! What is this?"

"Julie and her husband live in Little Italy. She brings fresh bread three days a week." The microwave dinged, he turned to pull out her plate, piled salad on it and shoved it in front of her with a look that dared her to argue.

Shrugging, she poured the dressing on and dug in.

"How do you feel about Gabe being gone so much, baby?" Nick asked as he got his own plate and sat down beside her. He knew the answer of course, he could feel it through their bond.

"It's his job."

"That's not an answer to the question, Tracy," Gabe said with narrowed eyes.

"What do you want from me? I can't say anything supportive. I'm sorry. I don't like the idea at all! In fact, I hate it. It makes my stomach hurt to think of only seeing you once a month or a few days here and there each month. I want you all the time, every day. I want you to come home every night to our house. In our state. But it's your job and you love it and I don't want to make you feel bad."

"I'm going to tender my resignation."

Tracy goggled at him but before she could argue he shook his head and went on.

"I've been thinking about it since we sealed the bond. About how agonizing it would be to leave you so often. It's hard enough with no one really. But impossible for me to leave you and Nick for so many days a month. I don't want to. And I'm an Alpha of Pacific now, that's important. And right now, in the shadow of all this crazy shit with Sarah and Ben, it's more important than ever that we stick together and run Pacific right. I do love being the Mediator. It's a great job. But I can be a mediator in the legal world too. There are law firms in Portland and I can take the occasional mediation job for National when and if they need me. But my place is with you and Nick. That's where I want to be. Where I belong."

"But who'll be the Mediator now?" Tracy didn't want to let herself fully accept it until she'd worked it all through with him.

"I'm not the only Mediator. As you know, werewolves are constantly fighting and having issues with each other. I can't do it all. There are wolves on my staff who will do a fine job. And in fact, I think that my intention to resign and go to Pacific will help the Enforcer know that I'm not trying to challenge him but to get him to see just how dangerous Warren Pellini is." He looked at her carefully. "Does that work for you? You're the one who has to live with two Alpha wolves and two bodyguards."

"I just don't want you to give up something you love for me. I don't want to be the reason you walk away from something you've worked nearly twenty years for."

"You're what I love. The rest can be worked out. And I love the house we're renting but we need something bigger now that we'll have Trey and Derek there, and each of us will need some office space for Pack business."

"If we bought the house, we could enlarge the pool house, make it into a residence for Derek and Trey."

"Yes. But what about our children?" Nick said seriously and Tracy realized that she wasn't freaked out by the idea.

"We'll talk about some ideas once this is over."

Gabe grinned and moved toward her but the front door opened and Julie returned with Milton and Derek.

* * * * *

They decided to tackle the issue head-on. Nina had faxed over what she found but it wasn't as bad as they'd thought. The National Enforcer wasn't in deep to Pellini the way that Ben and Sarah were, thank goodness. They could catch the situation early and push Pellini out before he gained any more influence. Or so they hoped.

The National Pack house was in a freaking mansion on Beacon Hill. Tracy was blown away by the place as they entered through the front door. Templeton Mancini, the National Alpha, strode into the hall and swept Tracy into an embrace before she could say a word.

He kissed both cheeks, grinned at her eyebrow ring and looked her up and down before nodding and finally looking at Gabe with approval and then back to her with a wink.

"Hello, sweetheart! Congratulations to you. A tri-mate bond with one of my wolves, I'm very impressed and proud. You've got all the archivists atwitter, you know. Told me yesterday that yours is the first tri-mate bond in forty years. Welcome!"

Templeton was six-feet eight-inches tall and at nearly seventy, he was as spry as a man forty years his junior. He quite literally was the strongest wolf in the country and it radiated off him in a way that Tracy could feel physically. No one would be challenging this man and winning for a good decade or so.

He turned his attention to Nick and shook his hand. "Congratulations to you as well. On both your mating and becoming Alpha of Pacific. It's a heady thing, isn't it? You can feel all your wolves needing you, needing your guidance and strength. Some days it feels like a millstone, others like a true gift."

He strode over to Gabe and patted his back and hugged him. "I can feel it in you too. I think that this doesn't bode well for me and my Mediator." Templeton eyed Gabe carefully.

Gabe laughed. "I should have known. I plan to resign my position in National to take on membership in Pacific full-time. I can help out from time to time but I need to be near my mates. Need to run my Pack. But I want to talk to you about something before I resign officially."

"Okay. I'm anxious to hear what the story is with you all becoming Alpha. Come on through, the others are in the living room."

Gabe followed and Nick and Tracy walked in behind him. There were three other wolves sitting in the room and one female standing near the couch, who beamed when they entered.

"Gabriel! You've brought your sweet little mate." She rushed over and kissed Gabe and then turned to Tracy. "Honey, I'm Carla Mancini and we've been waiting for you for a long time. I can see the difference in Gabe already."

Tracy smiled. "Thank you. I'm the lucky one here really."

"Piffle!" Carla said with a snort. She eyed Nick and kissed him on the cheek as well and ushered them all to a couch. "You're a blue-blooded wolf from a fine, strong bloodline. Nick is as well and Gabe is incredibly strong and intelligent. You're going to make some amazing babies."

Tracy laughed then and took the drink Templeton handed her.

"Oh, where are my manners?" Carla turned to the two wolves sitting across from where Tracy and Nick were. "This is Jack Meyers, the Enforcer and Tina Elder, the Fourth."

Tracy gave them both the inclination of her head they deserved to be accorded by their rank and noted the warm smile Tina wore and the look of apprehension Jack had. She wished for a moment that she'd brought Shelley with her to flutter her lashes at him to catch him off guard.

"Please give Lex my regards. He's something else, your brother," Jack said and Tracy felt a bit more hope that perhaps he wasn't as far gone as they thought he might be.

"I will. He said you two met at some kind of training given by the FBI a few years back. He was impressed."

Jack's left eyebrow rose slightly. "It was a good training. Lex, of course, outdid everyone on the course. Damned excellent tracker, probably the best in the country." Belatedly his eyes moved to Nick and he colored slightly, making Nick laugh.

"It's okay. I know. Be glad he lives across the country from you and he's not your brother-in-law. It's a good thing I'm Alpha now, Lex casts a pretty big shadow." Nick was good-natured but still strong. Tracy liked that. He wasn't as serious as Lex had been before Nina.

"Man could get a damned complex from Lex Warden," Jack rumbled. All of the males laughed and the females looked at each other with amused smiles.

After they'd made small talk for half an hour or so, Gabe leaned forward in the way Tracy had come to recognize as his mediation stance. His body seemed relaxed, hands either loosely clasped between his knees or one holding a pen. But his eyes missed not one detail and she sensed the coiled-up energy in his muscles. He'd be able to spring in to action at any moment.

"What is it, Gabe? Speak freely." Templeton leaned back and crossed his legs.

"There's trouble in the Pack ranks, Alpha. I've been approached by several Alphas in many Packs nationwide, either in person or via phone, about their concern with Warren Pellini and his growing influence in National."

Jack's eyes narrowed and Templeton's body tightened. "Warren is a friend of Jack's, Gabe. Careful where you tread."

"Yes, sir, I know. And that's why I was silent for so long about it. But the numbers continued to mount and just recently, an issue came up that led me into a position where I can no longer remain quiet."

Templeton made a rolling motion with his hand to urge Gabe to get on with it.

"You're aware that Nick has ascended at Pacific, I know. But Pellini is the reason for it."

Gabe entailed the whole story to them, complete with the financial records they'd gotten on Ben and Sarah.

"I would have advised any wolf in this situation to come to you, Jack. That is, before you became so close with Pellini. And now I fear that I can't do that and that's what led me to finally say something. We can't have wolves feeling they can't turn to National for help. It is my sincere belief that any association with Warren Pellini and the Pellini Group is dangerous for us all. If the humans find out about the existence of a werewolf mafia, we are all at risk."

Templeton's face was an emotionless mask. "Is that all you had to say?"

Gabe was taken aback. "Yes, sir. I'd hoped we could work something out to help get Pellini off the back of Ben Lawrence and his kids so they could make their lives elsewhere and also to reassure the other Packs that National wasn't compromised."

"You intended to sever your Pack membership with National tonight?"

Tracy's stomach sank.

Gabe took a deep breath. "Yes. My mates are in Portland so my life is there too. I travel too much as Mediator to be able to be the husband I need to be. I can still help out on local mediations."

Templeton stood and held his hand out and Tracy and Nick followed Gabe, totally stunned.

"Thank you for your service, Gabe. You've done this Pack proud. Please look through your staff and recommend a replacement. And I advise you to speak no more about this Pellini situation. It could be detrimental to you and yours."

Tracy saw Gabe's outrage at the threat but even she felt the command in Templeton's voice.

"Sir, I will have to do what it takes to remove the threat of Warren Pellini from my Pack. He has broken laws that could incriminate my wolves. I can't have that. And I would never allow any harm to come to my mates without heavy retribution." He looked Templeton in the eye and both men stayed that way for several long moments.

"Leave that to me. Now go."

No one followed them out.

* * * * *

"Damn it!" Gabe's fist drove a heavy dent into the door of the apartment.

"I don't understand this. He seemed so nice. He can't be in on it with Pellini, could he?" Tracy led Gabe into the living room and pushed him into a chair while she went into the kitchen to grab a beer.

Coming back out again, she handed one to Gabe and then Nick and sat down, curling herself around Gabe. Sensing his anger and his hurt, she ran gentle fingertips up and down his neck.

"I don't understand it either. I've known that man for twenty years and he's never threatened me. I've never seen him do anything I'd ever describe as unethical. Not ever."

He sighed. "I may have to talk to an old friend who's gone to work at the Department of Justice about this."

Milton came padding into the room and put his chin on Gabe's knee. Tracy grinned and shook her head.

"You take the cake, dog of mine. You need to walk, dude?"

Milton barked and she stood up. "I'm going to take him out for a bit of a walk and to make a pit stop." She went to grab her coat and Milton's leash.

"Take Derek with you," Nick called out and Derek stepped into the hallway with her.

"Sheesh, it's cold out there. Don't make poor Derek schlep out into the night to go walkies with me and Milty, that's not fair."

Derek snorted a laugh. "Not a big deal, Tracy. I'm a werewolf, I hear they're pretty hearty."

She rolled her eyes at him and shrugged. "I'm a werewolf too, you know. You think some mugger or something is going to try and shake me down once I let my wolf take over and shift a claw with three-inch nails?"

"They're your mates, they want to protect you. It's in their genes," Derek said quietly and she sighed.

"Okay, come on then." Tracy knew he was right and she wanted Gabe and Nick to relax instead of coming out with her, they both had enough to deal with.

The night was quiet outside but Tracy could hear the sound of the T trains going over the river back and forth between Cambridge and Boston proper. Milton was in doggie heaven, sniffing every tree, every curb, every hydrant and car tire. He barked a few times, more because he could than anything else. She was going to have to take him to the park if they stayed in Boston any longer than the next day or so. Run him with his ball.

She was still ruminating on exercising Milton such that she didn't hear the screech of tires and the sound of running feet until she was already in the air and being carried.

She started her change, letting her wolf feed on the adrenaline of the moment. Milton was snarling and barking and she heard Derek's howl as she was shoved in a car.

"Do not change, Tracy, or we will be forced to kill the dog and the bodyguard. We've got a gun loaded with silver shot pointed at your head anyway. Be smart and listen."

Recognizing the voice as that of Jack Meyers, the National Pack Enforcer she'd met that very evening, she stopped the change. Breath heaving, she focused on him as the car lurched away.

"You know they'll hunt you down and kill you. Jesus, how stupid can you be? And Lex and Cade will come back here. You'll start a clan war, the first one in a hundred years. All for Warren Pellini's money? What the fuck is wrong with you?"

"Calm down for god's sake! I'm not going to hurt you, I just had to talk to you."

"And you didn't talk to me an hour ago at the Pack house why?"

"Tina is in it up to her stupid fucking ears with Pellini. She's a spy. Any reaction we gave you in front of her would have been reported back to him. Probably already has been. We've contacted some people who've gone to get Ben and to take him, Sarah and the kids out and to a safe location."

"Oh my god!" She scrambled in her pocket for a cell phone.

"Don't call the apartment, Pellini has been listening and watching you three. I'll get you back in another few minutes."

She nodded and relaxed a bit, hoping like hell Gabe and Nick weren't crazy with fear for her safety.

"Now, listen and listen carefully. I'm working with Templeton, a human cop named Stoner and an FBI agent named Koehler to take Pellini down. We can't be seen helping you, Tracy. Templeton did call Pellini and order him to back off Pacific, which he reluctantly agreed to do. But you can't tell anyone but Nick and Gabe about this. We've been working to catch him since the hit on your Third last year."

"Ben Stoner?"

"Yes. I forgot, he's a cop in your neck of the woods. He's been made a liaison between the Pack Enforcement and human law enforcement on this issue. The FBI agent is a wolf."

"Okay, so what do you want us to do?"

"Tell Gabe and Nick about this but not in the apartment. Write it down and then flush the paper. Don't say a word about it in front of anyone else. Pellini has spies everywhere. Then get the hell out of Boston tomorrow first thing. Hell, tonight even. Watch your back. We'll have some wolves on you to keep an eye out but don't let your guard down for a second. Pellini hates you, Tracy. Hates the Wardens and now he's sure to hate Nick and Gabe too. Stoner is going to head out to talk to Lex and Cade tonight about this whole thing, they're under threat as well."

"Crap. What the hell do we do? Other than watch out for a revenge-crazed werewolf don?"

Jack smiled despite himself. "Keep an eye out and ears open. Gabe will need to let a few tight-lipped comments about me drop here and there. It's imperative that Pellini continue to think I'm in his pocket. To keep cover, everyone else has to think so too. This money laundering stuff is small potatoes. He's got fingers in everything, drugs, prostitution, and we're very concerned that the lycanthropy virus may be in his hands still. He's crazy, Tracy. Bio-weapons in the hands of a man like Warren Pellini? It can't happen. And so I stay deep. And so you and other wolves the rest of the nation looks at for moral guidance must begin to break with me. Templeton will bear some of this as well but we can't afford to weaken him too much or he'll be challenged. Stoner will keep you all apprised as he can."

The car turned back toward the apartment building. "I can't be gone much longer, we shook a tail earlier but we have to let it pick us up again near my girlfriend's place. Luckily, she lives nearby. We aren't going to slow too much. Can you handle a roll to the grass strip at the curb?"

Tracy took a deep breath and nodded.

"Okay and one other thing, I'm going to have to rough you up a bit. I told Pellini I was going to send someone out to put a scare into you to get you the hell out of town. It has to look the part. I'm pretty sure you can trust your bodyguards but I don't know about the others in the building. It's a Pack building and other wolves live there."

"Okay. I suppose I'll heal."

He smiled again. "Ready to take one for the team?"

As she nodded he slapped her face, hard. And three more times, until she looked pretty swollen.

"I'm really sorry. Gabe is gonna kick my ass for this. Here comes the place, I'll open, we'll slow and you jump out. Tuck your shoulder down and roll. Be well and we'll be in touch."

It all happened very fast and suddenly Tracy found herself hitting the grass hard and rolling as the car screeched off.

Running footsteps and muffled voices greeted her as she tried to stand.

"Oh my god, Tracy! Are you all right?" It was Julie, looking horrified. "Get her into the building and up to Gabe's!" she snapped at two other wolves standing there. Tracy saw Julie talk into a cell phone and then close it and look back to her. "That was Gabe. He's frantic." Julie pushed the hair back from Tracy's face and winced.

The big wolf carrying her was gentle as they went to the elevators. Gabe and Nick burst out and both men froze at the sight of her injured and in the hands of a male wolf.

"I'll kill Pellini," Nick growled. "It was him, wasn't it?"

Gabe took her from the other wolf and told them all to go back to their own homes. Julie rode up with them and went to get tea and a cool compress for her face.

"Are you all right?" Gabe demanded, putting her gently on the bed.

Nick took off her shoes and Milton came bounding into the room and jumped on the bed, looking at her himself to be sure she was there and okay. "Hey pooch, it's okay, the gravy train is still kicking and ready to toss some table scraps your way," she said playfully and Milton whimpered and lay down next to her, much to Nick's annoyance.

"You've seen her, Milton. Now go and get in your bed. She's okay and I want to be next to her." Nick looked the dog in the eye and Milton started to growl but thought better of it. He licked her hand and face and she started to kiss him but winced at her split lip.

"Go on, sweetie. Momma will be okay."

He gave her one last lick and went to lie in his bed, propping his head on the side of it to keep an eye on her.

"What the hell happened?" Gabe demanded as he took the cold cloth from Julie and put it on her face.

She really felt that Julie was trustworthy but couldn't take the chance of being wrong. Too many lives were at stake. "It was one of Pellini's people. Said that we needed to get out of town or else. We need to go." She grabbed Gabe's hand and he saw the scrapes on her knuckles from where she'd fought as they pulled her into the car.

"Not before I hunt him down and kill him." Gabe's eyes had gone amber-gold and his voice was little more than a guttural growl.

She looked at Nick and said carefully, "We need to go. Now." She wanted very badly to tell them everything but she knew with Julie there and the way they were being watched she couldn't.

"Julie, can you help us get the bags packed, please? And do you suppose we could fly back in the Pack plane or are we bound for commercial air travel?" Nick knew she had something to say from the looks she was throwing him. It was clear she hesitated to speak in front of anyone else and so he went along with her.

"They want us gone. I have no doubt that they'll be willing to let us fly out on their jet. Julie, I hate to impose but can you call them first? We didn't unpack much."

Julie smiled down and stroked a hand over her hair. "Of course. It's not imposing, although I hate the idea of losing Gabe and now you. You aren't coming back are you? Something bad is happening."

"Yes. Yes, Julie, something bad is happening and I've resigned to run Pacific. You and Rick are welcome to come out west to join Pacific if you want to. There'll always be a place with me for you both."

Julie hugged Gabe. "I don't know. Our kids and grandkids are here."

"You may want to avoid Pack functions for a while. And watch your back." Tracy hated the lines of stress around Gabe's eyes. He clearly hated thinking Jack and Templeton were in cahoots with Pellini.

"Okay, Gabe. You be careful too, all right? Now I'll go make the call from downstairs and get everything prepared for your departure. I'll also take care of packing this place up and shipping it all to you."

She took one last look and left the room.

Tracy waited until she left and Nick started to demand an explanation but she put a finger over his lips and shook her head. She mimicked writing and Gabe nodded and went to the bedside table to find a pad and pen.

"I was worried sick. God, Tracy, when Derek came running back into the apartment without you I thought I'd die. Milton was barking and growling and inconsolable. I wanted to call the cops but we didn't know quite what to do. Gabe called Templeton, who said he'd get the word out. Oh shit, I suppose we should take care of that."

Gabe handed her a pen and paper and she began to write. She gave them the whole story on paper as the others made small talk as cover. Gabe called Templeton on his cell and said he thought Jack was involved in Tracy's abduction. Templeton told him that meant he should get the hell out of Boston.

Thank goodness for werewolf healing. Tracy was feeling a lot better forty-five minutes later when they were all ready to get to the airport.

"I packed you two suitcases, Gabe. Your suits are in two garment bags and already loaded into the car. If you're going to get a job out there, you'll need to look nice. Your everyday clothes are in the suitcases. Oh and I'm rambling, but I'll miss you. You've been like a son to me. Please take care of yourself and your mates." Julie wrung her hands nervously.

Gabe kissed her forehead. "You too. There's a place for you, don't forget that. Hell, for all of you if you want. Portland doesn't have nearly the humidity in the summer that we have here."

"But they don't have the Red Sox." She smiled sadly. "I'll think on it. I promise. Now go before I start crying."

It was nearly dawn by the time the plane landed in Portland, they heaved a sigh of relief. No one really spoke much on the flight, not knowing what was safe to say, or if the plane was bugged. Nick had plans to check the house over carefully for listening devices but Tracy felt on edge anyway.

They went home and Tracy checked in with Nina from her cell phone in the backyard while she tossed a ball with Milton under Gabe's watchful eye. Lex had apparently gone over the house with a fine-tooth comb before feeling satisfied that they weren't bugged. He'd also gone out and changed and went around the property in wolf form to track for anything unusual. Much to his annoyance, there was evidence of a place where someone had sat in a tree and watched the drive to the house. The scent was cold, but enough for him to double the guard and to bring Tegan to the house to live there. Poor woman, didn't even get three days at her new house.

Long after midnight, they crawled into bed and each other's arms. Nick was assured they were safe and free from listening devices but they couldn't trust everyone in the Pack.

Exhausted, each sought comfort rather than sex and both males were terrified of injuring her. Gabe itched to knock Jack out for putting Tracy in the middle of this brewing war. The fear of the news that she'd been taken still echoed within him, shocking him in moments where he thought he'd gotten past it. The helpless rage, the terror. He never wanted to feel that again. If he had to sit on her that's what he'd do to make sure it never did happen again.

Tightening his arm around her waist, he nuzzled his face into her neck.

Nick's mind raced. Fury rode him hard. He wanted to find Warren Pellini and end this himself. How dare he threaten his family? How dare he try and destroy his Pack? And Jack and Templeton? He growled and Tracy started and then stroked fingertips up and down his spine to calm him.

"I'm all right. I'm here," she murmured.

Damn right, and she wasn't going anywhere without him or Gabe until this was all over and done with. He wanted to rip Jack Meyers' head from his body for hitting Tracy. He knew it was necessary and all, but the way she'd looked when he stepped off that elevator, he'd never be able to erase that from his memory. Helpless, bruised and battered. Warren Pellini would pay for that.

Tracy felt her men at war with themselves. She knew it couldn't be easy for them to have seen her that bruised, for them to have endured her kidnapping and the minutes she'd been gone. Worse, she knew the fear of it happening again would make them stick to her very closely until this was all over. She'd be lucky if she got to go pee alone.

No, until this was over, she'd be watched like a hawk. Overprotected by her mates and surveilled by the fucking werewolf mafia.

Things were a long way from over. In fact, she had the distinct feeling that they were just beginning. Despite that part, she had Nick and Gabe at her side. And each day they worked to make the relationship better. Feelings would get hurt and territory would have to be renegotiated between the three, but their bond was solid, and healthy. And she felt love and belonging. It was complicated, belonging to two men, but worth it. And she still held out hope for more boy-on-boy action, as she quite often teased. Sometimes they gave her some. Ah, a girl is lost without hope.

Laughing, she pressed a kiss into first Gabe's shoulder and then Nick's. It would be okay.

Also by Lauren Dane

ಐ

Print Books:
Cascadia Wolves 1: Enforcer
Crown and Blade
Feral Fascination *(anthology)*
Sexy Summer Fun *(anthology)*
Witches Knot 1: Triad
Witches Knot 2: A Touch of Fae
Witches Knot: 3: Vengeance Due
Witches Knot 4: Thrice United

About the Author

ഌ

Lauren Dane has been writing stories since she was able to use a pencil, and before that she used to tell them to people. Of course, she still talks nonstop, and through wonderful fate and good fortune, she's now able to share what she writes with others. It's a wonderful life!

The basics: Lauren is a mom, a partner, a best friend and a daughter. Living in the rainy but beautiful Pacific Northwest, she spends her late evenings writing like a fiend when she finally wrestles all of her kids to bed.

The author welcomes comments from readers. You can find her website and email address on her author bio page at www.ellorascave.com.

Tell Us What You Think

We appreciate hearing reader opinions about our books. You can email us at Comments@EllorasCave.com.

Why an electronic book?

We live in the Information Age — an exciting time in the history of human civilization, in which technology rules supreme and continues to progress in leaps and bounds every minute of every day. For a multitude of reasons, more and more avid literary fans are opting to purchase e-books instead of paper books. The question from those not yet initiated into the world of electronic reading is simply: *Why?*

1. *Price.* An electronic title at Ellora's Cave Publishing and Cerridwen Press runs anywhere from 40% to 75% less than the cover price of the exact same title in paperback format. Why? Basic mathematics and cost. It is less expensive to publish an e-book (no paper and printing, no warehousing and shipping) than it is to publish a paperback, so the savings are passed along to the consumer.

2. *Space.* Running out of room in your house for your books? That is one worry you will never have with electronic books. For a low one-time cost, you can purchase a handheld device specifically designed for e-reading. Many e-readers have large, convenient screens for viewing. Better yet, hundreds of titles can be stored within your new library — on a single microchip. There are a variety of e-readers from different manufacturers. You can also read e-books on your PC or laptop computer. (Please note that Ellora's Cave does not endorse any specific brands.

You can check our websites at www.ellorascave.com or www.cerridwenpress.com for information we make available to new consumers.)

3. *Mobility.* Because your new e-library consists of only a microchip within a small, easily transportable e-reader, your entire cache of books can be taken with you wherever you go.

4. *Personal Viewing Preferences.* Are the words you are currently reading too small? Too large? Too… ANNOYING? Paperback books cannot be modified according to personal preferences, but e-books can.

5. *Instant Gratification.* Is it the middle of the night and all the bookstores near you are closed? Are you tired of waiting days, sometimes weeks, for bookstores to ship the novels you bought? Ellora's Cave Publishing sells instantaneous downloads twenty-four hours a day, seven days a week, every day of the year. Our webstore is never closed. Our e-book delivery system is 100% automated, meaning your order is filled as soon as you pay for it.

Those are a few of the top reasons why electronic books are replacing paperbacks for many avid readers.

As always, Ellora's Cave and Cerridwen Press welcome your questions and comments. We invite you to email us at Comments@ellorascave.com or write to us directly at Ellora's Cave Publishing Inc., 1056 Home Avenue, Akron, OH 44310-3502.

ELLORA'S CAVE

Romanticon

Annual convention
for women who
refuse to behave